Survivor

A novel

by

Tom Creary

Other novels by the author:

The Bohemian Connection (2013)

The Lady from Toledo (2014)

The Russian Intrusion (2016)

Sisters (2018)

The setting is serene, a quiet place apart from the bustling, everyday activity of the naval base. The gleaming white structure close to the shore of an island of Pearl Harbor, Hawaii, sits over the water and the submerged hull of the U.S. battleship Arizona, destroyed the morning of December 7, 1941. 1,177 men of the Arizona lost their lives that day. Whatever is left of the remains of over one thousand of them are still entombed in the ruins of the ship sitting in the mud just below the surface of the water. Set among those remains are those of 36 survivors of the 1941 attack who had their ashes lowered into the hull to be with their comrades following their own deaths many years later. A white marble plaque with the names of those who in death returned sits below the one covering the end wall, listing all those men of the Arizona who died that December day in 1941.

Chapter 1

December 6 1941, Honolulu, Hawaii

The sailors, soldiers and young women erupted with cheers as the band played the opening tunes of 1941 America's number 1 song, The Chattanooga Choo-Choo. "Pardon me, boy, is that the Chattanooga Choo-Choo?" "Track 29!" "Boy, you can give me a shine," sang the vocalists. As the sun set, the band played one after another of the popular big band tunes of the day: In the Mood, Moonlight Serenade, A String of Pearls, and many more. The floor was filled with young people dancing and enjoying that lazy, heavenly Saturday evening.

Bob Kane and Katie McLean had met on the beach that afternoon. A few hours earlier, as the 21-year old sailor lay on the sand with a group of buddies, he saw her walking, ankle-deep, in the water along the shore. Brown curly hair flowing gently in the warm breeze. Wow, thought the young man. He got up quickly, got in step beside the girl and made his intro. "Hey, you shouldn't be wearing those sunglasses. They're probably hiding the nicest parts of a pretty face." She slowed down, turned toward the young man, but before she could say anything, he blurted out "Can I walk with you? You're too classy to be walking alone."

"I don't know. You're pretty brash," Katie said as she took off her sunglasses and looked at him. "I suppose so, though, as long as you agree to buy me a coke when we get to the stand over there," adding playfully, as she sized up the young man who had just showed up with the awkward introduction. At that moment, she was not happy. She had a date to go to the open air concert that evening but the guy had a friend tell her the date was off. Off. No explanation. The friend would not say why. It was just off. Upset, she decided to walk down the beach and work off steam and now this guy shows up. Seems nice. Cute. Maybe he'll want to go to the concert.

"Ok. It's a deal. Where are you walking to? All the way down the beach?"

"All the way down and all the way back," she replied. "In the meantime, let's go get a coke."

"What's your name, by the way? Mine's Bob. Bob Kane."

"Katie. Katie McLean," responded the girl as she looked down the beach, seemingly preoccupied with something else other than a conversation.

"I'm from Kansas, by the way. Where are you from?" he asked.

"Missouri. St.Louis."

"You upset about something? You sure seem to be," asked Bob after taking a few steps alongside her.

"Yes, I am. I just got stood up by a jerk who was supposed to take me to the concert tonight. He really teed me off. No explanation. Had somebody come and tell me. What a chump. You going to the concert by any chance?"

"Why, yes I am, with a bunch of guys from the ship. But I can go with you, if you want, or, putting it another way, you can come with me."

Katie turned around, looked at Bob, hesitating a moment before responding.

"OK, you seem to be a nice guy. I do want to go, but that's all this is about, OK? We agree to go to the concert, nothing more. Got it?"

"Sure. Whatever you say." Hey, I've already got a date with her, he thought. They continued walking along. "And what are you doing here in Hawaii? Nurse, teacher?"

"I'm a nurse. Military hospital. And you. You must be a Navy man. Said you were on a ship."

"Yes, Navy."

"What ship are you on?"

"The Arizona. One of those big ones over in Pearl - the flagship of the fleet," Bob responded proudly.

The two reached the coke stand, found a raised table under a parasol, sipped their drinks, then walked back to where Bob had left his things, all the while talking and trying to get to know each other. His buddies were whistling as the two approached from the edge of the water. "Hey, Kane, what you got there? Wow! You win, you win, you win" as two of them waived their white navy issue towels.

"What's that all about?" asked Katie as they approached the group.

"A little game they play every time we come to the beach. About who meets the prettiest girl."

"You say the game THEY play? You don't play it?" Katie asked mischievously.

"Well, it's kind of hard to say I don't. But please don't be offended. I'm really glad I met you and I look forward to taking you to the concert tonight. Never mind the game."

Katie McLean was getting to like the sailor from Kansas who had an engaging smile, a quick wit, and a soft manner about him. And Bob Kane was already smitten with the smart, beautiful girl he had met but an hour before.

He grew up on a farm outside the small town of Silver Lake, Kansas, near the state capitol of Topeka. The 1930's were tough on farm families in Kansas and just about everywhere else as well. The depression and the ravages of drought had taken took their toll. In 1936, when Bob was sixteen, his father lost the family farm to the town bank, as he had no way to pay the mortgage. The drought of 1935 and 1936, what became known as the Dust Bowl, had turned the soil of the Kane farm to dust, with much of it literally blowing away. It became impossible to feed the livestock or even the family over time. The few cattle and hogs the family had managed to keep were sold off one by one for whatever they could fetch at the town's auction. One day the local bank manager showed up with the order. The family lived for the next few months in a small apartment above the general store on the town's main street, in exchange for Bob's father's helping out in the store.

Bob's mother never got over the loss of the farm and died six months later. His father ended up taking the only paying job he could find, at a meat packing plant in Kansas City, seventy miles away. He had to leave his four children behind until times got better. The two girls, thirteen and twelve, were placed with a sister in Wamego, and Bob and his brother Johnny, fifteen, with another sister in Topeka. Times did not get better and the family never did reunite under the same roof. Bob finished high school and was accepted to attend college with a partial scholarship to play football. The balance of the costs not covered by the scholarship, was paid by an uncle of his mother, who had always taken a liking to the young man. He spent a year at the University of Topeka, a time that he loved and would cherish all his life. However, it was not to last. The day after Bob turned nineteen, early in the summer between his freshman and sophomore years, his father was diagnosed with cancer and was dead within six weeks.

While his father was dying, Bob was informed by his uncle that he could not support his college any further. He was losing his insurance business. Clients could not make their payments. Bob would have to manage on his own. His time in college was over. After the death of their father, he and Johnny decided to enlist in the military, in the Navy. "Join the navy and see the world" said the recruiting posters. That is exactly what the Kane boys wanted to do - get away from the barren fields and destitute towns of Kansas, the loss of their parents as well as the lack of any opportunity that was available to them. See something else; start a new life. "Navy here we come," said Bob to his brother as they left the recruiting office that late summer day in 1939.

Kathleen "Katie" McLean had spent her own early childhood years on a farm as well, near Hannibal, Missouri. At the age of eight, her father, tired of farming the land he had inherited from his father, sold it to a neighbor and moved the family to St. Louis where he took a job selling heavy machinery. Her mother, who had been a teacher in Hannibal, easily found a teaching job in St. Louis. Times were good in 1928, but by 1931, her father was unemployed and the only income the family had was her mother's meagre teacher's salary. It took two years before her father found other work. Katie vowed to have a profession that would always be needed. At twelve years old, she decided she would be a nurse. There would always be work for nurses.

Bob and Katie did not share family histories that afternoon or evening. They never got to it. The time was in the present. They danced to every tune the band played that evening - all the popular ones of Glenn Miller, Tommy Dorsey and Harry James. America was not at war; it was a long way off on the other side of the world. Things were good. Hawaii was paradise, particularly for two 21-year old kids from the Midwest who had grown up in the hard times of the '30's.

Chapter 2

December 7, 5:30 AM, on the Japanese aircraft carrier Hiryu, 275 miles north of Oahu.

Captain Keiji Hakagawa was exhorting his men. "We are attacking the American fleet at Pearl Harbor. We will be crippling America's might in the Pacific. Japan will reign supreme. Over 350 bombers and fighters will be in the attack. We will be flying over the island of Oahu, down the central valley to the harbor on the south side. Here is a drawing of the placement of the ships we are to destroy. Our target is the battleship Arizona. We expect heavy interference from American planes and anti-aircraft fire, but we must persevere. There will be no going back once we reach our destination." He finished with the exhortation "May the gratitude of our nation fall upon your shoulders and bathe you in glory and honor for all time. Be brave, be strong. For the Emperor. For Japan. Go forward, warriors, towards victory and honor forever!"

Keiji Hakagawa, age 24, was a reluctant warrior. He liked Americans and had spent time in America. In the lead up to the hostilities, he had been against war but kept it to himself, avoiding shame on his family. He was the son of a decorated naval officer who had commanded a destroyer in the First World War. He was a top student throughout his youth and learned

English on his own. He spent two years studying aeronautical engineering at the University of Oregon, before graduating later with honors from Tokyo University. He had learned to fly at 18 and in 1938 joined the military to continue the family tradition. He was sent to the Imperial Navy's aviation officer training school, where he was soon slated to be a bomber pilot. In the spring of 1941, Keiji was placed in charge of a torpedo squadron stationed on the aircraft carrier Hiryu. War with America was coming. He knew it but did not like the thought. He had enjoyed his time in the United States. He had made many friends there. He did not like what was coming, but followed the family tradition to be a good, loyal officer and warrior in respect of his father and allegiance to the Emperor.

He had prepared himself to die. The crews to take part in the next day's attack were told they may not come back. "Many of you may die today. Be proud. You will be heroes to our people, our nation," Hakagawa said as he concluded the briefing.

Before reciting a prayer and catching a few hours sleep, Keiji wrote a letter to his wife. "Miko, my dear companion, I am prepared to die. With honor. It could happen tomorrow, or the next day, or the next day after that. You will have received this long after our actions in the days ahead, which you know I cannot tell you about. I have never wished to kill. You know that. It is not the reason for me doing what I am doing. I have a duty to carry forward the honor of my family and must live up to that. I am a warrior as my ancestors have been. I serve the Emperor. It is my destiny and my duty. I love you. May you live a long and productive life after I am gone. Whatever happens, you have my enduring love forever. Keiji"

The first planes launched at 6:30 AM. At 7:45, Hakagawa's squadron reached the coast of Oahu without incident, along with 135 other torpedo bombers. Forty-five of the B5N's held one 1720 pound armor piercing bomb each. Their targets, to be attacked from 10,000 feet, were the battleships. Other B5N's had smaller torpedoes that would be launched along the water towards the battleships and other ships in the harbor. As they approached the target, Keiji realized there were no American planes in the air. No opposing aircraft. No American plane anywhere, he thought as they reached the coast just before 8 AM.

"Tora, Tora..." heard Keiji over the radio. Total surprise, he thought, as he saw the first series of explosions on the airfields and on the water where dozens of warships were anchored, unsuspecting and without cover. No anti-aircraft shelling. Nothing coming up. *Total surprise*. Breaking radio silence, he exhorted his men: "Warriors. Arizona below, at two o'clock, second from the right. Kaga goes first, we follow in order : 1 to 4. I will go last. Acknowledge visual recognition. Glorious warriors of the Emperor, attack!"

7:25 AM, on the Arizona..

"What a night last night. Billy, I'm in love."

"So, the chick from the beach has you already. That was fast."

"Yep. She sure has. I'm in love. I was awake half the night, just thinkin' about her. Can't wait to see her again" replied Bob as he and his buddy Billy Riley were sitting in the galley deep inside the ship, eating a bacon and eggs breakfast. "I've been awake since 5 o'clock."

"Some babe, Bobby boy. Whew. The bathing suit. The hair blowing in the wind. You really struck it, man. Lovely. How did you do it? You're a pretty quiet guy."

"My down-home Kansas ways, my friend, plus my humility. She said so. And my football build."

"Your football build? My ass."

"I'll have you know I played tailback at Topeka U. Started. She was impressed."

"Did she know what a tailback was?"

"Not sure, but hey Billyboy, you got to admit I'm a pretty handsome guy. Close to it anyway."

"Right. You just lucked out. She got stood up and you came along. That's what you said last night, anyway."

"Destiny. It happens."

"Did you kiss her?" asked Billy mischievously.

"All right, all right. Back off. Of course, I kissed her, but it's none of your damn business. I can only say it will be the first of many.....What about you last night?"

"I ended up dancing with four different girls. All part of a group Davey, Jimbo and I met. They went to the concert by themselves - nurses and secretaries who just got here. Not one of them showed any possible lasting interest in me, however, and it was mutual. But I had a great time. A few beers. Probably a couple too many. Got to the ship just before curfew. My luck will change one of these weekends, Bobby. Just as long as we don't ship out. What's your lady do? Where's she from?"

"She's a nurse. From St. Louis. I'm gonna see her next week."

"If we don't ship out."

"Yes, if we don't ship out."

Billy Riley got up and placed his tray on the gurney next to the table. "Well, I'm off. Need to go down to signals. Some settings to check, part of the routine. Then to my bunk for some more shuteye. I don't have to be anywhere this morning."

"I'm going up on deck." responded Bob. "Don't have to, but I got to do something. I'll take up a mop or something, whatever. Need to get the thoughts of her out of my mind. At least for awhile. See you later. Maybe we can play some cards up on deck later."

"Good idea. I'll be happy to take some money from you. My turn. You practically cleaned me out last week. Say goodbye to your paycheck, buddy! See you at noon." Billy went through the bulkhead at the end of the galley and Bob found the staircase to the decks above.

Bob Kane never saw Billy Riley again.

7:50 AM on the deck..

Bob Kane, Seaman First Class, Signals and Communications, was on the deck, washing the turrets of the big guns in the stern area of the huge battleship, and thinking only of the girl he had met the day before. Washing down guns was not

17

his responsibility - he was a signalman - but he needed to do something. He was one of forty or so men above deck at the moment he first heard the noise of aircraft engines coming from the north. The noise was getting louder, much louder. Lots of planes, he thought. What's going on? He looked in the direction of where the roar was coming from and saw a swarm of planes fast approaching at low altitude from the valley. What is this? Who are these guys? Our guys on exercise?

The first torpedoes hit the water. Explosions. Ships being hit. Not our guys. We're being attacked, for Christ's sake. Bob could see explosions at the airfield on the north side of the harbor. He turned left, away from the airfield and saw a plane skimming across the water, coming directly at him. Its guns were blazing, bullets soon hitting the conning tower and railings, ricocheting everywhere. Men were being hit, some falling into the water. The plane flew right over where Bob was, veering right over the end of the stern at the last moment to avoid slamming into the ship. Red circle. Japanese. Shit. They're all over the place. Where are our guys? Bob Kane was not a gunner but managed to get to one of the antiaircraft machine guns and worked feverishly to get it working. The ammunition boxes were not open. Canvas covers were over the guns. How could we not know about this? We are sitting ducks. Bob took the cover off, pried the ammunition box open, fed the cartridge belt into the magazine; all of it taking up precious time. We're not ready for this. Damn! Bullets were hitting all around him. He managed to turn the gun around to face another incoming fighter, but it would not fire. Bob frantically tried to get it to work, while calling out for help. The gun would not fire. Somehow he managed to avoid getting hit. He looked around. Men were streaming on to the deck, running everywhere, frantically trying to reach their battle stations. He did not know it, but over 1200 of them were still below deck, many in their bunks, and most would never make it out, dead or alive. He saw the big unmistakable frame of Jimbo, Jimbo from New Orleans, the fun-loving joker of his group of buddies, scaling one of the ladders up the side of the conning tower, suddenly being hit and falling back on to the deck. Five minutes into the attack, the Arizona had been hit by three bombs launched from the B5N Kate torpedo bombers, damaged but not crippled. The fourth one and the one that would doom the ship and the men inside was soon to come. Explosions were erupting everywhere. Seven of the eight battleships lined up along Ford Island had been hit already, along with other ships alongside and in other areas of the harbor. Johnny. His ship over there next to the California. It's on fire. Oh, no. Johnny. Bob had last seen his brother the night before on the other side of the dance floor. They had waved to each other. What's happened to him? God damn these Japs!

As men streamed on to the deck from below, they were cut to pieces by the strafing Zero fighters. As the first bombs rocked the ship, men, wounded and screaming, were being thrown into the water. At 8:06, the fourth bomb hit, a 2,000 pounder launched from Hiryu torpedo bomb squadron plane number 4 from ten thousand feet. It knifed right through the deck plating just inside the bow into the ship's munitions storage area below deck, igniting a million pounds of gunpowder. In a few seconds, the huge explosion rocked the ship, causing it to rise out of the water, all 35,000 tons of it, then fall back, tilting sideways, mortally wounded. Known as The Pride of the Fleet, the flagship of the U.S. Pacific Fleet, the biggest battleship of the American navy when built in 1915, was burning, exploding, finished. Hundreds of crewmen trapped inside died instantly. Others who survived the explosion but were stuck below would burn to death or drown. It would take only four minutes for the huge battleship to sink into the mud of Pearl Harbor. The fires inside the ship would burn for two days. Neither the men trapped inside nor their remains would ever get out.

The explosion threw Bob into the water, his head hitting a piece of metal. The water was on fire. He found himself next to a patch of burning oil, with debris, bodies and parts of bodies floating around him. Dozens of men were close by in the water, many with their faces and heads burning as they screamed. Bob saw a man trying to hold on to a piece of debris but with the half-melted skin of his arms dripping off of him. Other men still alive in the water and able to swim were frantically trying to get away as the burning ship listed sideways, steadily sinking into the mud, sucking everything around down with it. He saw a plane coming over the water, flying right over the wreckage, right over where he was, in the water off the stern. Not firing. Why not? He's still got his bomb. He's going to drop it. He's not doing it.

Bob frantically swam away from the burning ship, somehow avoiding the patches of flaming oil. His head hurt. He managed to reach the island alongside the ship, and collapsed after reaching the shore and lifting himself out of the water.

The plane that flew over the wreckage and the huge clouds of black smoke rising high in the air moments after the big bomb that destroyed the Arizona had hit was Captain Keiji Hakagawa's. The ship was tilting, on fire, sinking. Parts of bodies littered the water. Men were burning as they struggled to free themselves from the flames, from the debris crashing around them. Fighters strafed the water, finishing off many of the men who had managed to flee the burning, sinking ship. But he was not firing. He was not proud. He thought he should be - his men had accomplished their objective - but he was not. He was appalled at the carnage he was seeing. He dropped his bomb into the water, away from any of the burning ships below. As he gained altitude for the return voyage, he had a sense of foreboding.

I will have to confront this someday in my life. It will happen.

He also realized at that moment that he was not a warrior. I cannot do this again, he said to himself.

Upon his return to the carrier, he was commended by his commanding officer. Two days later he received a medal conferred on him personally by Admiral Isoroku Yamamoto, the overall commander of the Japanese attack forces, as the flight commander responsible for the sinking of the Arizona. But Captain Keiji Hakagawa was a shaken man, appalled at what he had seen. He could not get it out of his mind.

The extent of the destruction at Pearl Harbor quickly became known by the battle group as it retreated away from Hawaii. Four battleships sunk, four others damaged, fourteen other ships sunk or seriously damaged. Details of the American losses, including the destruction of the Arizona received from Japanese intelligence agents on the island, were shared with the officers of the attacking squadrons. The reports cited intercepted US Navy communiqués that hundreds of crewmen of the Arizona were dead or presumed dead with the complete loss of the ship. Hakagawa was viewed as a hero, but he did not feel that way. He was shaken by the carnage of what he had seen. He barely managed to hide it from his men and his fellow officers.

Chapter 3

Bob regained consciousness two days later in hospital, his head and arms swathed in bandages. "You hit your head. It'll heal, but there's a crack and it will take some time. You will have headaches for awhile. Your arms will be OK. Some scars definitely but they will be OK," said the doctor. Bob had trouble concentrating. His head seemed to be in a vise. His arms hurt. What happened to the guys? Where is everybody? Billy, Davey. Billy going down to signals. Who got out? How could this have happened? Nobody knew they were out there? This is crazy.

The doctor came back the next day. Bob had questions. The nurses had been too busy to talk. Badly burned guys, far more badly burned than he, seemed to be in every bed. Attention was on them.

"Doc, I need to know some things. Can we talk?"

"You should not be talking much. Your brain needs a rest."

"But I need to know what happened. What happened to the ship, to my buddies? I have a brother on another ship."

"What ship were you on?" asked the young doctor.

"The Arizona."

"The Arizona. Bad. But not the time to talk about it, sailor. You just rest and get well. Don't need to know anything else right now. You were lucky. And you have no damage to any of your organs, your spine, eyes or ears. Your head is scrambled a bit, but you should get through it OK. We just have to be careful about it. We will keep you here for awhile."

"Doc, the ship. Bad. What is bad? What happened to it?"

"Not operational anymore. Lots of men lost. That's all I know right now. But there is nothing you can do about it. You need to focus on getting better."

"Not operational. I don't know what that means. Lots of men lost. How many is that?"

"Sailor, I can't tell you that. I don't know." He did know, but he was not going to tell him. At least not now. The truth was devastating. Over half of the losses in the attack that day were from the Arizona, still burning and leaning to one side, half submerged in the harbor.

"Ok. About the headaches. They're terrible. How long will I have them? I can hardly stand it. All the time. Every moment. I can't stand it, Doc."

"They will go away. Takes time. You have a fissure in your skull. Your brain took a jolt. It needs time to heal. Take the aspirin. It will have to do, but not too much of it. Four tablets max a day. I can't give you anything else."

"OK. Something else, Doc. I need a favor. My brother. John Kane. He was on the Shaw, the destroyer tied up next to the

California. I need to know what happened to it and to my brother. Any way you could find out what happened to him?"

"I'll try. John Kane. The Shaw. I'll have somebody look into it."

"Thank you."

"Rest, Kane, rest," said the doctor as he left to look into other head injuries down the row of beds.

Bob Kane learned a few days later that over 1150 of the men on the Arizona had died. It was something that no one wanted to announce or admit to. But it was not unknown in Hawaii. He was told there were only 300 or so survivors, with most of those seriously burned, wounded or crippled. A few days after that he learned that most of the dead were still in the remains of the ship, with little prospect of their bodies being recovered. He could not stop thinking about it. It enraged him. All those guys, gone, trapped inside. He tried to find out if his buddies Billy, Mike, Joe from Chicago, Davey, guys he had trained and crewed with, survived. Probably not. Their bunks were deep inside the ship. Billy, where are you?

The next day, a lieutenant he had never seen before came and told him that he was sorry to report that his brother, John Kane, was not among the known survivors of the Shaw. The ship had exploded and many of the crew were still missing in action and presumed dead.

The bastards. I will get back at them, if it takes forever. They will pay for this. I am going to fight them, fight them, fight them. For you, Johnny. You didn't have to follow me. I brought you into this. Little Johnny. Promised Dad I would look after you and I brought you to this.

The nightmares came. Billy and Mike waving their towels on the beach. A shell exploding where they were standing. Gone. A plane with the red circle on its wings screaming low over the crowd and the orchestra on the stage, machinegun firing, musicians getting hit, instruments flying into the air. Fire consuming the dance floor. He would wake up in a sweat, yelling, with guys in his row looking at him.

While wondering about Johnny, about his friends and whether they were dead or alive, he thought of Katie. Where is she? Was she OK? He had heard that a military hospital had been hit with loss of life. Was it hers? He had never asked her that night what hospital she was working at. Please, God, not her too.

Three weeks later..

Katie had been at her new hospital for three days. She was looking at the clipboard. It had the list of personnel being treated on the third floor burn unit. Her floor was the second, but she had been asked to fill in that day on the third. Seaman Robert Kane, Bed 62. Bob from Kansas was not dead. He's here.

Bob saw her as she walked down the aisle, looking at him. She broke into a smile as their eyes met.

"Katie, not the place where we were to meet again. Not exactly the beach," said Bob with a big smile on his face below all the bandages as Katie came alongside his bed.

"You're alive, Kansas boy."

"I guess I'm lucky. Not many of us got out. I guess you avoided it as well. I heard a hospital got hit bad."

'Wasn't mine... How was it, Bob? It must have been horrible. Your ship was the worst hit."

"Yeah, it was. Lots of guys gone. It was horrible. We didn't have a chance. The whole thing exploded, rose up in the air, I was thrown into the water. Burning oil, parts of the ship in the water, flying in the air, landing all around, Japs strafing the water, fire everywhere. I hit my head bad. I don't know how I managed to survive."

"I tried to locate you afterwards, but I had your name wrong. I was looking for a Robert Cain, C-A-I-N. No record of anyone with that name in any of the military hospitals. I thought you were dead, one of the guys still in the Arizona."

"Well, I'm not dead and I'm really glad to see you. I had a great time with you that day. I was looking forward to doing it again."

"Yes, doing it again. That would have been nice," said Katie. Bob sensed hesitation in her voice. Something was missing.

"Where were you, Bob? How did you get away? So many did not."

"It was incredible. Horrible. I could not believe what I was seeing. We were totally unprepared. I was on deck, thinking of you, by the way," as he looked directly into her eyes, "doing something that I was not even responsible for. I needed to do something. I first heard the planes, a roar coming in over the water, then I saw them - hundreds of them. I tried to get a machinegun going but it wouldn't work. For them, it was easy. Like rabbit hunting with my dad back on the farm - just like it. So many rabbits in the snow on the fields we just picked them off. I had the same thought when I saw the Jap planes speeding through the harbor and shooting everything in sight. Guys cut down everywhere. They had no chance. We had no chance."

Katie hesitated a moment, as she appeared to search for words. "I'm glad you're alive. You know I really enjoyed that Saturday night. It's like years ago, but really it's been just a few days. The whole world seems to have changed since then." She looked at Bob, at his bandaged head and arms before continuing. "You have a head injury. Burns as well. What do they tell you?"

"Crack in my skull. Should heal OK. Burns on my arms. I'll live. Are you going to be my nurse? That would be nice if you could." Bob was hoping that could be the case. He would see her every day. But he could sense that all was not right. Not the same spontaneity, the same current between them. Something had happened. She came back the next day to talk with Bob and the next day as well. But by the end of the week, she was gone. The nurse on duty said she had been transferred to another hospital that had been converted from a hotel. A few weeks after last seeing Katie and before he had a chance to track her down, he was put on a ship for Seattle for the completion of his recovery. Beds in Hawaii were at a premium, needed for treating casualties coming in from other Pacific bases that had been attacked in the weeks following Pearl.

It would be months before Bob would have any news of the lovely, energetic girl he had met the day before his life had changed. He would only learn in time that three days after the attack, Katie had met someone at the hospital where she was working, an officer. She had assumed that he, Bob Kane, was dead. Just about everybody who was on the Arizona was dead. By the time she discovered Bob in the hospital in January, the relationship with the officer she had met was beyond return. They would marry in March 1942 in a hastily arranged ceremony before he set sail with his ship for Australia and the long campaign to retake the key islands of the Pacific.

In the meantime, before leaving Hawaii, Bob found one of his friends from the Arizona.

He thought he knew who everybody was on his floor, and none of them were guys he knew beforehand. But this was definitely the voice of Davey, Davey Poole. The joker, banjo player and everybody's favorite guy from Tennessee. He got up from his cot and went down the row to the far end. The man with the bandaged face and head with openings for the eyes, nose and mouth with the unmistakeable voice of Davey Poole was yelling at the nurse next to him. "I can't see anything! I can't smell anything!"

"You will, it'll come. The swelling around the eyes will subside. Your eyelids were burned. They need to heal, and they will. Your eyes will be OK. The doctor told you that."

"Can I believe that? Can I really believe that? I can't. The skin on my face is all burned. It will be one big scar. I'll be a freak. I don't know if I want to live. I want to die. Will you help me die?"

At that moment, Bob arrived at the end of the bed, announced his presence. He had heard the conversation. "Davey, this is Kane. Bob. I'm here, at the end of your bed."

"Bob Kane? Bobby. You're alive. And you're here too. I thought you would be gone, along with all the others."

"Not dead, Davey. And you aren't either. Nurse says you will see again. What's this stuff about not wanting to live? You have your eyes, your ears as far as I can tell, and your arms, hands and legs. Hey, man! You're going to live. They are telling you that. What is this stuff about wanting to die?"

"You sound like a preacher, Kane. You don't know it all. I'm burned over 80% of my body."

"Ok, Davey. We need to talk. Really need to talk. You are alive, and that's what counts. They've told you that you have all your limbs, your eyes, your ears. With all of that, there's a full life out ahead of you, man. Come on."

"Bullshit, Bobby. I'm going to be a freak."

"Listen, I'm coming down to see you tomorrow when hopefully not as many people will be around. If need be, I will have you rolled to the sun porch at the end of the hall. We'll talk about things. Alright?"

"About what?" asked Davey

"About you and what you're saying and about being alive."

Bob came back the next day. He started right in. "Davey, I heard you telling the nurse yesterday you didn't want to live. What is this bullshit? All for a bunch of scars?"

"Bob, what are you doing? Giving me a bad time? I have enough of a bad time."

"Listen. You may not realize it, but you are a lot better off than a lot of the guys on this floor and you still have all your parts. You can't see the guys, but I will tell you about a few of them."

"I don't want to hear about them. Why are you doing this, Bobby? I don't need your pep talk."

"Oh yes, you do. I will finish what I was saying. The guy over across from you and two beds down has no legs and only one hand. The kid six beds down from him has lost both of his eyes. His nose has no skin or cartilage. One of his ears melted. The guy six beds down on the other side lost an arm and a leg and is messing an ear. He may not see again. You are lucky, Davey. We are lucky. We will be able to work, to live, with all of our faculties. Those guys and many more on this floor will have a difficult time of it. So, can the talk."

"I'll be a freak. Scarface. No girl is going to want to be with me, Bob! Nobody is going to want to hire me."

"Patience, man. They've told you you will be alright. Limbs, eyes, ears. So what about scars. Nobody will see them under your clothes. The face, so what. People will just have to get used to it. Enough for you to want to die?"

"Go back to your end of the floor. I don't need this."

"Yes, you do. Coming back tomorrow. I'm not letting you out of this."

Bob rose from the side of the bed, took a few steps toward the aisle, then said to his old buddy, "In a week or so, you will be able to see, as I understand from the nurse, and you will be able to observe what a babe that nurse is. You can begin to work your Tennessee charms on her."

"I don't want to hear about it," said Davey.

"Wallowing in pity. Such a waste. You have a lot going for you, Davey. You were the smartest guy in the unit, slated for officer school and all. Best bluegrass picker in Pearl. You still are that guy. Whether you like it or not, I will be back tomorrow."

Later, Bob was in the sun room at the end of the hall where men who could walk and get around were allowed to go and sit after meals. He was talking with another man with head bandages, with an arm in a sling.

"What ship were you on?" asked the other man.

"The Arizona. What about you?" replied Bob.

"The Utah. Lost a lot of friends."

"Yeah, me too. Just learned how many are dead. Over a thousand guys. Unbelievable. Many buddies gone. One of them is here, though, and I'm working on him. Bad burns everywhere but he has all his faculties."

"Oh yeah, the guy at the end of the row with the bandages on his face and I guess everything else. I saw you with him earlier."

"He was a pretty handsome guy, smart as hell, damn good banjo player. Can play just about any instrument. Fastest guy to learn the signal codes of anybody in the Navy. Sure of that. He thinks his life is over. Gotta pick him up."

"What about you?" asked the other man.

"Crack in my skull that will take some time to heal, along with some second degree burns on my arms. I will be OK, despite the headaches. And I'm going back."

"Back to what?"

"To the war. To kill as many Nips as I can. Davey Poole, the guy with the burns and my buddy, will not be able to do it, but I will. Pay back time."

"You really want to go back. You won't have to. Head wounds can get you a medical discharge with honor."

"My honor will be when I manage to kill as many little fucking Japs as I can. The war has just started and I'm going to be in it, beginning just as soon as I can get out of here."

Bob Kane spent close to an hour with Davey Poole every day for the next two weeks before leaving for Seattle. On the last day of his time at the hospital, he observed his friend, now with the bandages off his eyes, laughing with the nurse. He thought he could discern the beginning of the making of a pass at the nurse. I think he's going to be OK.

Bob Kane and Davey Poole would remain close friends the rest of their lives.

Chapter 4

Seattle, Washington, early February 1942

"Here they come! Here they come!" Bob woke up in a sweat. The same nightmare. Bob Kane was itching to get out of the hospital and back into service. He could not stand to observe guys anymore with parts of their bodies missing do their best and sometimes not their best in dealing with their conditions, like his good friend Davey back in Hawaii. He also could not bear the thought of spending another afternoon playing cards. He had no more headaches. His burns were just about healed. Have to get out of here, he told himself every day.

The administrator had Bob come to his office. "Kane, you can leave now. You're OK. The doctors tell me the crack in your skull has healed. There should be no further issues with that. I gather you haven't had a headache in over a week. Your burns were only second degree with no nerve damage or anything serious. You're good to get out of here. You can continue in the navy if you want or you can receive a medical discharge. Tell me what you want to do, now or we can talk about it tomorrow. No rush. Not many men in your condition have this choice. You do."

"Captain.....Sir....I can tell you right now. I want to fight. I want to stay. Some unfinished business to take care of. I was on the Arizona. I need to get back into the line of duty. I have a score to settle." Bob didn't say anything about the nightmares.

"OK. You know you don't have to. You can get a discharge, but if you want to stay in, you're welcome to it."

"There is one thing I would like, however. I would like to do it as an officer. Would I be eligible for officer candidate school?"

"Well, I have your file here. Let me see….Graduated from high school. Top grades. One year of college. Good grades as well. Says here you had to drop out because of lack of funds." The navy captain read on. "Your naval record is clean. Signalman. Very good reports. You just may qualify, Kane." The officer looked at Bob, then continued. "Here's what you do....."

Two days later, First Class Seaman Robert Kane was being interviewed by a Navy staff officer. "Why do you want to be an officer, Kane? By the way, how old are you?"

"I'm 21, sir. Is that too young?"

"Almost. But you've been in the Navy for two years. It helps. Now why do you want to be an officer? I hope it's not because you want to give orders, rather than take them."

"Sir, I have never had a problem taking orders. I want to be an officer to have a greater say in this war. I want to pay the Japanese back for what they did. I want to lead men in doing that, with increasing responsibility over time. I see myself being more useful in that as an officer. I have done my bit as an enlisted man. I believe my service record is a good one. I believe I have more to offer, Sir. I hope the Navy can see that in me."

"Sounds good, Kane. Your service record is a good one, by the way. Commendations all up the line. I am putting in your application."

Bob returned to Kansas where he was assigned to work as an inventory administrator at a naval air training center near Kansas City. It could not have been a more boring job. Far from where he wanted to be. But he was in line for officer training. It kept him going.

One day his aunt received a letter from the Navy. "Johnny's dead, Bob. They found his remains. He is buried in the Honolulu military cemetery at a place called Kanuahu. Letter is signed by the Secretary of the Navy."

"He never made it. I knew it that day. All my fault. I brought him with me. I promised Dad I would protect him, look after him. I didn't."

"You did what you thought was right. There was nothing here for either of you. No jobs. No way for Johnny to go to college. For you as well. Nobody knew the war would be coming for us. It was all about Germany and England and France. So far away. You couldn't know we would be in a war three years ago. Bobby, you taking Johnny with you was the right thing to do. He had nothing here."

"All I know now is that I am going to get back at them. I have no interest in just quitting and coming back to work here or anywhere else while those little s.o.b.'s out there inflict pain. I'm going to get many of them before I'm finished."

"Kane, why are you so damn angry all the time?" asked the lieutenant in charge.

"I guess you don't know that I was on the Arizona. I survived and more than a thousand of my mates, including many of my friends, did not. I am angry. I have a right to be. I just want to be able to exact some revenge. Give some pay back. They got my little brother as well. Stocking shelves here does not get me there. That in itself is enough to make me angry. They could have given me an assignment related to signals, which I know something about. A lot about. But they didn't. So here I am, a bored and angry man. Sorry about that, Lieutenant."

"Understand. Hopefully, you can exact that revenge soon. I understand your application to OCS is moving forward."

"Good to hear. Thank you for sharing it with me. I need to get out of here, Lieutenant."

"Like I said, understand. In the meantime, could we talk about that day? Pearl? The Arizona? Do you want to talk about it? You're the only one around here who went through that," asked the Lieutenant.

"No, I don't. It's enough thinking about it. Sitting up in the middle of the night. Sorry, Lieutenant, I really don't want to talk about it. If you don't mind."

"Understand."

On the weekend, back in Topeka, Bob was with his aunt on the porch of her house.

"Bob, you are so melancholy. There is no joy anywhere in you. Ever since you got back. So morose."

"Aunt Barbara, I am alive. Those other guys on that ship, and Johnny, are not. They're gone. Why them and not me? It eats at me. All the time. I survived. They didn't."

"You can't change that. You can't feel guilty about being alive. You have to make the best of your life. It's just beginning. You just turned twenty-two. And this wanting to go back. Do you really need to do that? You've done your bit. You gave the Navy over two years of your life. You almost lost your life doing it. You lost your brother. You need to cut away from it. And stop feeling guilty about surviving."

"I can't. I need to do it. I would not be able to live with myself if I didn't. Like my old high school buddies, Jimmy and Skeet, when we went to play pool last night. They have no idea of war, although they are certainly going to be drafted, probably soon. They could not begin to understand my feelings about going back. They think I'm crazy. They said I was lucky. I'm not lucky, Barbara. I'm a mess and I have to get it out of me. That can't happen here." He paused a moment, then continued. "It's revenge. I know it. But it eats at me. I see those Japanese planes in my sleep every night. I have to do it. I do feel guilty at being still alive. Sure. That may never change. But I have to go through with this. If they approve me for officer training, I'm going. And if they don't approve me for that, I may go back anyway. Ask for an assignment somewhere in the Pacific, be part of the fight."

"Bobby, you will surely die doing it. So wrong-headed. You've served your country. You've done your bit."

"No, I haven't, Aunt Barbara. Not yet. I'm not finished. If I quit now, I will never be able to live with it."

Two months later, on a day in October 1942, Bob Kane was on a train from Topeka to Chicago, where he would spend the next three months at the Navy's Midshipmen's School on the campus of Northwestern University.

Chapter 5

June 5, 1942, on the carrier Hiryu near Midway Atoll, 1,200 miles northwest of Hawaii

Planes coming in. Not supposed to be here. They're not ours. Get in the air! Keiji Hakagawa had received his orders in the attack of the American carriers, believed to be 120 nautical miles to the east, but the roles were in reverse. It was they who were being attacked and his crews were still below deck, preparing to take off in an hour. He had to get to his plane. He located his gunner somehow in the frantic activity, grabbed him, and raced to the lead torpedo plane prepared for takeoff. They got in, strapped themselves in their seats with Keiji frantically beckoning to the deck crew to release the cables and turn the propellers to start the plane. The engine sputtered to life. Bullets from the American planes were hitting the deck all around as he spun the plane around for take-off. Men racing to their planes were being hit and falling. Planes behind him were being hit. Two were on fire. Keiji's torpedo bomber rumbled down the runway, past other planes and crews scrambling to take off. The plane with its two 550 pound torpedoes barely managed to get off the end of the carrier with enough momentum to avoid crashing into the sea. Keiji got the bomber aloft. Four Zeros managed to get aloft as well before the carrier was hit by torpedoes launched from a swarm of American planes. *This is what we are supposed to be doing - attacking their carriers. They are doing it to us. How could this be?*

Of the ten bombers that were to make the run, his was the only one in the air. He would go to the target zone per his orders - planes from the other carriers would be joining in - but before turning east with the Zeros rising after him, he looked back down to the right. Explosions on the carrier. Columns of black smoke rising in the air. The ship tilting as fire consumed the deck crammed with planes readied for flight with tanks full of fuel. He watched as two planes slid off the side and into the water. At that moment, bullets tore into the fuselage around him. He felt a pain in his leg. He had been hit. American planes were everywhere in the sky. The Zeros were badly outnumbered. Two of them were already hit and going down. As Keiji tried to stabilize the plane, the engine stopped turning and caught fire. He was going down. He managed to get out despite his wound and parachute to the water. His gunner was not so lucky, trapped in the plane as it plummeted to the sea with the torpedoes still attached to the underside of the fuselage. They exploded on impact. Keiji floated along in the air and landed within sight of his burning carrier, and was rescued soon after by a crew from an escort destroyer. His active service would be over. His leg was badly injured, with the femur shattered in three places. He could not walk without the aid of crutches for close to a year.

In May of 1943, fourteen months after Midway, he was re-assigned as a flight instructor where he remained until the end of the war.

In the three and half years between March 1942 and the end of the war, Keiji Hakagawa was celebrated as one of the heroes of the attack of Pearl Harbor. The picture taken at the ceremonial award of his medal by Admiral Yamamoto was used by the Navy with the picture reproduced and sent for posting throughout the Navy. It was also posted throughout the country, in schools, hospitals and public buildings. Keiji Hakagawa was a hero. But he did not consider himself one.

"Miko, I am disturbed by this. All of it. I am not a hero. I saw what I did, we did. What my men did. Many, many men dead. I did not want to kill. I saw them. It turned my stomach. I was ashamed that day. I still am. And I saw many of our own men killed a few months later when we were attacked. We lost more men that day than the Americans lost at Pearl Harbor. Over three thousand. I am not a hero. We are losing the war. All this has to stop. It should never have started."

"You have said this before. I understand. The end of the war hopefully is near. You have done your duty . Your honor, Keiji, is untarnished. Your father is proud of you. You don't have to tell him any of this. Life must go on. And it will." Two months after this discussion with his wife while he was on leave, the atomic bombs fell on Hiroshima and Nagasaki, leading to Japan's surrender five days later. The war was over.

Chapter 6

February 1943

A little over a year after Pearl Harbor, Bob Kane graduated from the U.S. Navy Midshipmen's School in Chicago. He had the rank of Ensign and was promptly sent to amphibious craft operations training at Baltimore, Maryland. He was to command one of the new LCT troop landing crafts, specially designed for landing troops and tanks on beaches in the Pacific. His ship and hundreds of others would form part of a task force charged with spearheading the landing of Marines at Pacific islands overrun by the Japanese. Many of those islands had to be re-captured. Three days before leaving Baltimore for Mississippi and the commissioning of his ship, Bob was at the base officer's club when he saw an officer across the room who he recognized from Hawaii. Who is that guy?....Yes...the administrative officer at the hospital. Maybe he will know what happened to Katie.

"Lieutenant, excuse me, but I remember you from Hawaii. The hospital where I was."

"Yes, Ensign, I was stationed at one of the hospitals there. My time as a paper pusher. What can I do for you?"

"Well, it's something personal. I'm trying to locate a nurse who worked there for a while. I had met her the day before the attack, then we saw each other at the hospital where I was. I lost track of her. Thought you may know what happened to her. She just disappeared from the hospital one day, and then I got shipped back stateside."

"Sure. Be glad to help. What was her name?" asked the lieutenant.

"Kathleen McLean. Everybody called her Katie."

"Yes, I knew Nurse McLean. She was one of the best. We moved her around to train new teams in the other hospitals we had to set up. She must still be in Hawaii. I believe she got married a few months after the attack. Many guys were disappointed about that. She was a pretty girl."

"Married. Oh." Bob was crestfallen and could not hide it.

"I see you are disappointed. I can understand. She was quite a girl. Lucky guy who got her."

"Thank you, Lieutenant. I wish I were that guy. Damn the war. Damn the attack. We had something going."

"Yes, damn the attack, but we will win this. Sorry about the news about the girl." The lieutenant observed the disappointment in the eyes of the junior officer in front of him. He tried to change the subject. "Where are you going now? Long way from Pearl here."

"LCT Group. Down in Mississippi. Leaving for the Pacific in a couple of weeks."

"Good luck, Ensign. Get a few Japs for us."

"Thank you, Sir. I will. Yes, I will do that."

Married. I knew it. It was all very different. She had met somebody. She was the one. Katie, oh Katie.

Ensign Robert Kane, with the crew of his LCT 1259 and the crews of four dozen other LCTs arrived off the coast of New Guinea in mid-October.

Somewhere in the Pacific, late 1943

"Kane, you're the only one in this unit who was an enlisted man before becoming an officer. Most of these other guys are college boys. I need you to be the voice of wisdom in this group. Not one of them has ever commanded men before. You have been on the other side. You know what it's like to receive orders from an officer, who could be the same age as you or even younger. I need you to be the leader of this group, the source of wisdom."

"Sir, I came back to fight. I will lead men, and I will do my best to inspire and provide example. I consider it part of defeating the enemy. Part of eliminating as many of them as we can."

"Well, Ensign, you better get used to being an officer that does more than kill people on the other side. There's more to it than firing shots at the enemy, as you well know. We deliver the guys and the tanks to do that. That is our focus. I need you to be an influence around here and to look after your men. Together and with the grunts we land on the beaches we will beat the enemy. Understand?"

"Yes, sir. I will do that, Sir."

A good man, Kane. But has a chip on his shoulder. Not good. I will have to watch him, thought the group commander as Ensign Kane saluted and left his commander's quarters.

That night and many nights during the war as well as afterwards, Bob Kane had a nightmare. There were different versions of it. Sometimes it was his brother burning, other times it was his friend Billy, other times somebody else. Burning as they walked on deck, with holes in their heads, then falling into the water, disappearing. It would not go away. His roommate would sometimes ask what was wrong, what he was dreaming about. "Fire on the farm when I was sixteen. Almost killed me. Still gets me. It's what these scars are about." He wanted no one to know he was a survivor of the Arizona. Why was I spared? Why Johnny, Billy, Joey, the others gone and not me? He would never be able to answer that question. His answer always fell on revenge. But it was not in his nature. Bob Kane was a gentle guy.

He and his crew were soon to see action, landing Marines at Bougainville in the Solomons in November. From there, they participated in other operations in a host of bloody invasions. LCT 1259 would land troops at the Admiralty Islands in February 1944, then move up the chain towards Japan. One of the links in that chain was Saipan.

Chapter 7

Saipan, Mariana Islands, June 1944

The incoming fire was deadly, raking the front of the boat. Bob could not see where it was coming from. The vessel was scraping the bottom a hundred yards from the beach. The other LCTs moving forward were stopping and lowering their landing doors. He had to do the same. It was not supposed to be this way. "Sand bar. Damn it." As the Marines rushed into the waste-deep water, machine gun fire ripped into them. Men were falling; the ones who were not hit struggled through the water, supported by fire from the landing force, planes from the aircraft carriers strafing the beach and the shelling of the tanks that were being unloaded and moving forward in the shallow water. The guns of the fleet supporting the invasion continued to pound the shore and the high ground looking over it, filled with Japanese artillery and machine gun nests, giving some chance to the Marines trying to make it to the beach and the foliage beyond. Where were the Japanese? I can't see any of them.

"God damn it! Where the hell are they?" yelled Bob as his machine gunner on the bridge raked the shore. Gunfire was coming from the jungle, but there were no Japanese to be seen. Bob could see fire coming from the sides of hills not far from the beach. "Caves, they're in caves, goddamn it."

"Sir, we need to get out of here," yelled Davis, his second in command. "Need to go back and re-load with more men. The tide is going out. We will be stuck if we don't."

At that moment, his gunner was hit. A bullet in the forehead. Bob had to take control and continue firing while his crew tried to disengage from the sand. A burst of fire caught another one of his men as he was raising the landing door. Another sniper's bullet grazed Bob's shoulder. He continued to fire into the foliage on the shore one hundred yards away. "You bastards! Here's for all my guys!" Bob's craft never managed to disengage from the sand bar that morning. After a few minutes, Bob could fire no more. The machinegun was out of ammunition. He and the remainder of his crew hunkered down and awaited the rising of the tide for them to disengage. In the meantime the battle raged. After awhile, Bob slowly rose up to look out over the water. It was pink. Bodies everywhere. Tanks landing on the beach were having trouble avoiding the bodies. The Marines who had made it to shore were moving inland, slowly, using grenades and flamethrowers. Planes continued to strafe the foliage. Between strafing runs, the cruisers and battleships pounded the inland area. When the tide finally came in, Bob's LCT disengaged from the sand. The un-damaged engine fired up and he and his remaining crew returned to the transport ship. As they receded, they passed bodies lolling forward then back amid the waves as the tide rolled in. "Damn it all. They never had a chance. The fucking Japs," Bob said to his 2iC. "They will need to pay for this. All of it."

It was the next day after landing more troops and equipment on the beach that Kane had an incident that could have got him court-martialed. Earlier that morning, he had lost two other members of his crew to sniper fire. He was still boiling with rage as he stepped over their bodies. As he did so, he noticed a group of captured Japanese soldiers being brought to the beach with hands tied, which was rare, as the Japanese rarely let themselves be captured. Raging at the loss of the guys lying below him, he went to the machinegun and turned it towards the beach and the captured soldiers fifty yards away. His second in command saw what was happening and yelled to him, "Sir, what are you doing? You can't do that! Stop!" Ensign Davis managed to reach the gun in time. He grabbed the barrel of the gun and raised it as it began to fire. "Sir, they are unarmed! Under escort. You can't do this!"

"Damn it, Davis! Hill and Shaughnessy. They're dead. Right here! Snipers. The bastards. That's four of our guys we have lost. I can't accept any more of it."

"Sir, you can't shoot those prisoners."

"Get out of my way," replied Kane as he sought to regain control of the machinegun.

"Sir, don't make this mistake. You could be court-martialed. Guys on the beach who are guarding them would see the whole thing. Sir, I can't let you do this."

Bob Kane managed to get control of himself. He looked at Ensign Davis, then turned away to look out over the water. He's right.

"You're right. Hill and Shag are gone, but shooting prisoners is not something we should be doing. I know that. I was losing it. Thank you."

"Sir, there are people who saw this. Guys over there are looking at us. This will get to the commander. What do I say if they ask me?"

"Tell them the truth; that I almost lost it and came close to shooting some prisoners. You talked me out of it and I listened. The truth, Davis."

Lieutenant Robert Kane was very nearly brought before a tribunal. In the end, it did not happen. He was reprimanded, but because of his exemplary service record, the leadership he had demonstrated since arriving in the battle zone eight months before and the recognition of the stress of battle, he did not lose his command.

"I told you when we started this, Kane, that you would have to temper your desire to kill. You almost lost your commission and you could have gone to jail. You need to thank Davis for stopping you. There is no mention of this in your service record. I have seen to that. We need you. Just cool it on killing Japs all by yourself. Any other thing like this and you are out of here. Understood?"

"Yes, sir. Understood."

Bob and his LCT participated in other operations on the way up to Japan. They saw action at Tinian in July 1944, Morotai in September, Mindoro in the Philippines in December, and the bloody battle for Iwo Jima in February 1945. He and his crew were involved in the last of the amphibious landings of the war at Okinawa two months later. By that time and despite the incident at Saipan, he had been given responsibility for a full squadron of LCTs.

The Okinawa invasion was the largest amphibious assault of the Pacific War and the most costly of all, with over 50,000 American casualties. Japan was determined to halt the American advance and turn the tide of the war. Okinawa was to be defended at all cost and to the last man. Bob Kane and his crews saw many men die. The landings were bloody, with the first waves involving Kane's LCTs under intense fire. Many crewmen in his squadron were killed, as the Japanese raked the invading forces with mortar and machinegun fire. The ferocity of the three-month long battle and the realization through it of what an invasion of Japan itself would entail was the principal reason for the use of the atomic bomb to end the war two months later.

Throughout his service in the South Pacific from 1943 to 1945, Kane had managed to keep from his crew and everyone else the fact that he was a survivor of the sinking of the Arizona. He knew he would not have been able to bear the questions and any discussion of that day, the day that had changed his life. Only his superior officers knew, from his service record. None of them ever asked him about it. Asked a few times about the scars on his arms, he said, just like when his roommate in hospital asked him about his nightmares, they were burns from a barn fire on the farm when he was sixteen. "Saved the barn and my favorite mare."

Kobe, Japan, October 1945

Bob was assigned to be part of the occupation of Japan after the surrender and sent to Kobe, where he was responsible for managing public services for a section of the city. The responsibilities involved coordination of the provision of food, water, and electricity as well as basic health care in cooperation with what local authorities had remained functional at the conclusion of the war. The city had been the target of many air bombardments that year, including a devastating firebombing in March and others later as the war came to Japan itself in 1945. The city, the sixth largest in Japan, with a population of well over a million, had many aircraft manufacturing plants and other war-related factories. They were prime targets and received multiple bombings from American B-29's. Another fateful element of Kobe was that virtually all of the buildings of the city were made of wood. The city was a tinderbox. The firebombing on the night of March 16-17 1945 completely destroyed an area of over 20% of Kobe's urban area. More than 650,000 people had their homes destroyed, and the homes of another million people were damaged. Later bombings of Kobe's industrial plants merely added to the carnage and the wasteland that the city had become. Into that wasteland came Lieutenant Robert Kane, U.S. Navy, in September.

"I hate these people. I have no sympathy for them. I'm supposed to provide for them. I can't do this, Bill." Kane was with his immediate superior in what had been converted into the officer's mess of the American occupation forces from a small private school in the center of Kobe.

"You have to. We have to. There's no getting around it, Bob."

"These people hate us. We hate them. You see the looks on their faces? Despair, hate. Mostly hate. They've been fire-bombed. Their homes are gone. Half of them live in rubble. Half or more of their families are dead. No men are around. Just old men, women and kids. They all hate us. We don't speak their language. They don't speak ours. The war's over. This job is not for us, it has to be somebody else. Bring over the social workers. We're warriors; we've been through hell. We can't do this. I can't stand it. I just want to kill the first Japanese man I see."

Bob hesitated a moment, then continued. "You know what I did the other day? I came across a middle-aged man in the street. Looked to be a proud man, walked upright. I gave him a nod and said hello in English. He said nothing. No bow, no nod. Nothing. He just kept walking past me. Then I said to him, certain that he would not understand, "I hope you are happy with all this. You people started it. You brought it on. The men of Japan are crazy. I saw thousands of them. Dead. Alive. Coming out of caves. Animals."

"He turned, looked at me, then said in perfect English. 'We were destined to do this.' Then he walked away. I can't stomach these people. I can't do this, Bill."

"It's not in your nature, Bob, just like anybody else doing this, to kill anybody or do what you say you feel like doing. You're not a killer. We're not killers. The war has done it to us. Use the sensible half of who you are. We have to do this. Part of winning the war. Get over the revenge. Get over it and do what you need to do. It's part of our task now. We won the war. This won't last forever."

"I don't know if I can. Beyond me. December 7th is still in my blood."

Three weeks later, Bob formally requested a transfer back to the United States, which would mean a decommissioning from active duty. His request was granted. Lieutenant Robert Kane landed in Seattle in December 1945. He would officially exit from the Navy in January.

"What are you going to do, Bob?" asked his superior officer after telling Bob his request for transfer had been approved.

"Return to Kansas to start with, although not sure of what is there for me now. I don't know. I would finish college if I could find a way to pay for it. Will need a job somewhere although I have no idea what it would be. I'll see to it when I get there."

"You could stay in the Navy if you wanted to, even with your request for transfer. So many officers are leaving. Leaves a lot of space for guys who want to stay, make it a career."

"Nope. I'm out. I've had enough. I don't know what I'm going to do, but sticking around is not in the cards," responded Bob.

"I've heard the government is in the process of setting up a program to allow veterans to go to college."

"Oh, yeah?"

"Yep. The government would pay for it. I'm told it's coming."

"Well, if that's the case, I would do it."

"Check it out when you get back."

"I will. Thanks, Bill."

One month later..

"Hey, Bob! Bob Kane, it's me, Irene, from Honolulu, the hospital!," barked the young woman in uniform as she crossed the courtyard of the naval base. Bob turned and recognized the nurse who had treated him in Hawaii. "My God. Irene. Yes. Of course I remember you. You took such good care of me. How are you?"

"I am fine. And you, an officer. You were not an officer then, I don't believe. Good gosh. Look at those ribbon bars on your chest. Where have you been?"

"All over. Places I will never want to see again. I went back into it all, went to officer training and all that. Needed to get back at them. Long story. Not sure it was the best thing for me to do, but anyway.....Being de-commissioned this week, by the way. Back to civilian life. And you, Irene, you look great. What are you doing here? Going home, out of the Navy like most of us?"

"Going home. Tomorrow. To Minneapolis. Getting away from it all. So glad it's over. Can't bear to see another broken body."

"Neither can I. Seen too many of them. Good to see you, though…." Bob was getting ready to continue on his way across the quadrangle to the officer's mess, but had a thought. *Maybe she would know something.* "Irene, wait. I have a question for you."

"Sure, Bob, what is it?"

"You remember Katie McLean, one of the nurses on our floor for a few days after the attack? She was great with me. But just up and left one day. You know what ever happened to her?"

"Yes. Katie. I ended up working with her a lot. She got moved around to help set up new hospitals. I was with her at two of them. She's still in Hawaii."

"Somebody I ran into after my officer training who was in Hawaii at the same time I was, told me he thought Katie was married. Did she marry?"

"You had a crush on her, Bob Kane. It's written all over you. Well, she did marry a guy, an officer, a few months after the attack. But he's gone. Killed at Leyte in '44. Went down with his ship, she was told. Katie's a widow. She's at Hospital 240 up in Kaneohe, at least as of a couple weeks ago when I last saw her. It is soon to be converted to something else, by the way. So, if you want to get in touch with her, do it soon before she moves on or some other guy comes along. She was devastated after her guy died, but it's been two years. Contact her."

"Thank you, Irene. I'm so glad we've run into each other. I am definitely going to contact her. I had met her the day before the attack. I really fell for her."

"So you did. As I said, it's written all over you."

"We spent the afternoon and later that evening together at that big concert on the beach. It was great. Saw her after - at the hospital - but it wasn't the same. She had undoubtedly met the guy. Maybe I can get it going again. Just like the day before that day. Thank you so much for this."

"Bob, if it doesn't work out with Katie, call me in Minneapolis," said Irene playfully with a smile and a wink. "Here's my folks' number there. I could get to like you. All the best."

"Yes, all the best, Irene. I'll see about Katie. If it doesn't work out, you just may see me," replied Bob with a big smile as he hugged the lady who had just given him a glimmer of hope.

Some light in the gray of the uncertain world he was going back to, of what he would do now after his war, his war of retribution.

"Oh, Irene, one other thing. Davey Poole, whatever happened to him? Remember Davey, the burned guy at the end of the ward."

"Yes. Davey Poole with the burns. He's OK I hear, despite what he went through. Back in Memphis. We kept him in Honolulu for a year before sending him back here. He ended up in Memphis. He was from Tennessee to begin with. There's a VA hospital there. It's been over four years since Pearl. He's probably out. The Memphis VA would probably know where he is. I have to go, Bob. All the best. Good luck with Katie."

That evening, Bob wrote two letters, the first one he wrote was to Nurse Kathleen McLean, care of Military Hospital 240, Kaneohe, Hawaii. The second one was to David Poole, care of the Memphis Tennessee Veteran's Hospital. Three weeks later, back home in Topeka, he received a reply to the first letter.

Dear Bob,

I was so happy to hear from you. I am so glad you are alive. So many people I knew are gone. I never thought I would hear from you again. As you said in your letter, the last time we saw each other was when I was filling in at the hospital. You must know, Bob, that I really liked you that Saturday before everything happened. I was looking forward to seeing you again. But just after the bombing, I met a guy who was nice, and fun, just like you. I fell for him. Then I saw you at the hospital. I didn't know what to say. I never thought I would see you again. You were on the Arizona and we all knew there were few survivors.

You made it, and I am so glad. Life has moved on in the meantime.

You said in your letter you went back to fight again. I admire that, Bob. So many guys never wanted to see any of it again. You can't blame them. You asked if I was married. Well, I am not married now, although I was. I married the guy I fell for. But I am a widow now as he was killed in '44.

You want to know if we can somehow see each other again. I would be glad to see you. I am going back to the mainland for a few weeks before I leave the Navy and return home to St.Louis. I will be in San Diego at the Naval Hospital there, starting March 15. There are three navy hospitals there. I will be at the biggest one, the one right on the beach I am told. I will be working there until the 1st of June. If you are around San Diego or St.Louis later on, I would be glad to see you. Let me know. I will be here for another four weeks.

All the best, Katie

Chapter 8

Kyoto prefecture, Japan, February 1948

Keiji Hakagawa, former naval officer, aviator, squadron commander and hero of Pearl Harbor, flight training instructor, was no longer interested in having anything to do with aviation, with airplanes, with military matters, with leading men, with anything remotely connected to the war, to the navy, including the military heritage of his family. His father had died a few weeks after the end of the war. Keiji had no more obligations to defend. He was committed to leading an entirely different life.

He managed to find a job as a science teacher in an elementary school in a small town not far from Kyoto, where he had grown up, and one of the few cities of Japan that had been spared by the Allied bombing. He was fortunate to get it as he had no experience in education, other than in instructing young men how to use their aircraft to kill people, and towards the end of the war, to kill themselves as Kamikazes. All of the previous male teachers at the school had volunteered or had been drafted for the war effort and would not return. They were all dead. He did have a university degree in engineering, though, and it was enough for him to be designated as the science teacher. He would be the only one for the whole school. There was no one else available. With a limp from his shattered leg that he would have for the rest of his life and a longing for a peaceful, humble existence with his wife Miko, who was pregnant with their first child, Keiji began the rest of his life far from everything he had lived before.

Teaching science to impoverished, generally under-nourished 10 and 11 year olds in the devastated, broken-down world of post-war rural Japan soon proved to be a frustrating and unrewarding experience for the former military officer.

One day toward the end of his second year of teaching, he was visiting Kyoto with his wife and daughter at the home of his mother. A few blocks away from his mother's home in an area of the city he had never visited before, he came across the entrance to a Shinto shrine. He stopped and looked toward the darkened interior of the elegant, wood-beamed structure. He had an urge to go in. It was not something he had ever felt before. Keiji had never been a religious person and had never felt the need to visit a shrine. His life had been all about studies, about succeeding in life, about engineering and practical things, about being a military officer in the service of his country. He prayed when times were rough, before going into battle as most military men did during the war, but prayer was far from being a daily routine. His parents had not been religious, although they revered the Emperor - a deity, a kami, in the culture of Japan. Something was compelling him to enter as he peered at the entrance and the shadows within.

"Why are you here?" asked the middle-aged priest who emerged from the shadows. He had observed the young man with the limp and a cane as he slowly moved around in the public area of the shrine. He watched as the man stopped a number of times, momentarily looking at the floor and then at the ceiling, eventually coming to the railing separating the priests' quarters from the public space, all the while looking somewhat bewildered. The priest surmised that the man had been in the war and was perhaps carrying the scars of it, most probably in spirit as well as in body.

Keiji had not seen the priest approach and was startled. "Oh, I'm sorry. So sorry. I should not be here. I am disturbing your peace. I'm sorry." Keiji bowed to the priest and turned to leave.

"No, no. Please do not leave. There is nothing wrong with you being here. You are welcome. Can I help you? Is there something I can do for you?" The priest could tell that Keiji was affected by something, was caught up in thought, something that he had interrupted. The young man was not at ease with his intrusion. "I am sorry. I intruded on your thoughts. Please stay here as long as you wish."

"Thank you. Thank you. But I must leave. I am so sorry." Keiji bowed, turned and left the shrine.

"Miko, something happened to me this afternoon. I had an urge to go into a shrine I was walking past. Something I have never felt compelled to do before. When I was there, I felt peace. A deep feeling of peace. Very strange. Very strange, my dear."

"Were you alone? Was there anybody else there?" Yes, something had happened that afternoon, she thought. It was in his voice, the way he described it.

"A priest. He startled me. He was very kind, though. I left quickly after he approached me. But I want to go back. I will tomorrow. I will see if I have the same feeling again. Quite strange. Compelling, even."

Keiji went back the next day. There was an elderly couple sitting in the corner praying but rose and left a few minutes after his arrival. After slowly walking around in the public area in front of the railing leading to the inner quarters, he sat down on the raised floor and crossed his legs. Within seconds he observed the priest coming around the end of the railing. The priest bowed slightly in Keiji's direction, then approached as the latter rose and bowed in return.

"You have come back. You are welcome to pray, to stay as long as you wish. We close the doors at 9. In the meantime, you may wish to light a candle over there. For any one or all of the lost souls of Japan." The priest observed Keiji and surmised he wanted to ask a question.

"I don't really know why I am here or why I have come back. I have never been religious but something came over me yesterday. I felt compelled to return. I felt a great peace."

"Do you wish to speak about it? I am here. You are free to share your thoughts with me, if you wish."

"Yes, I do, although the thoughts and the reason for me coming back here are not really clear. Forgive me. I do not want to take up your time."

"You will not be taking up my time. It will be well spent if I can be of assistance to you. Come with me. This is the public area, supposed to be quiet for visitors and worshippers. We will talk inside. Follow me."

"Please have some tea. Feel at ease. There is no one around here this afternoon," the priest said as they sat after entering the private quarters of the shrine.

"Thank you. You are very kind." The priest poured the tea, then addressed the young man seated in front of him on the raised matted floor. "You have pain. From the war, I believe and not just your leg. How can I help you?" asked the priest.

"I am ashamed of what I did. I should not feel that way, but I do. I was an officer, a commander of a squadron of torpedo bombers… Keiji told his story.

"I received a medal from the fleet commander. A picture of me with the commander was circulated throughout the Navy and throughout the country. I did not feel good. I managed to keep that feeling to myself throughout the balance of the war. It was a difficult thing to do - everyday exhorting young men to be efficient killers - while being appalled at it at the same time. You see, my father was a high ranking naval officer. I had a tradition to uphold. I could not, would not humiliate him by any action or word that would caste suspicion on my commitment to victory and the glory of Japan. I have difficulty with that to this day. It disturbs me still, even as the war has been over for two years. It is why I am here, in the end."

"I see."

"Yes, that is why I am here. But I don't know what to do about it now."

"What do you do now? How do you live? How do you earn your living?"

"I am a science teacher in a small primary school in the country. I don't have to work. My family has landholdings. My father came from a wealthy family and had managed to acquire much land through marriage and opportunities as they arose over time. I could sit back and just be a landholder, collecting rent. But that would not be productive. I have a cousin on Kyushu who does that. He is like a parasite. I don't want to be like him."

"I see."

"I leave the landholding business to my mother as long as she is alive. I teach to occupy my mind, my days. But it is not rewarding. My heart is not in it. Poor undernourished 11-year old country boys have little scientific inspiration in this devastated country. Their families are preoccupied with survival. Teaching in that environment is not easy. I am sorry. I have told you too much. Boring details about my family and my frustrations with teaching."

"No, you are not boring me."

"In any case, I guess I am in search of meaning in this life. The war devastated so much of what we are and who we are."

The two men paused and refilled their cups. Keiji wanted to know about the man in front of him. He had said a lot about himself. Could he ask the priest to talk about himself?

"You are a priest. Has this always been your calling? May I ask that?"

"Certainly, you may ask that. I have been a priest in our religion for ten years now. Not a long time, but a good time. Earlier in life I was a teacher of history. Japanese history at the University of Tokyo. My son caused me to change. War. In China. He was killed. He was our only son - brilliant, kind, an engineer. He was supposed to build bridges. The exuberance of our war leaders caught him, though. He became something else. A monster. The last time we saw him before he went back to China in 1937, he was no longer the kind, gentle son we knew. He had become a boasting, loud giver of orders and criticisms of all people who were not sympathetic to Japan's conquests of other peoples. He was something else. I was not happy with that. When we were informed he was killed in China, I left my post at the university. I was like you. I decided to devote my life to peace and the spirit. I was older than you when this happened, but I did it and I am grateful. I have no family left. My wife died in the bombing of Tokyo late in the war. The shrine where I prayed and worked was destroyed that same night. I came here after that. This is a modest shrine. You must know there are over 400 Shinto shrines in Kyoto. This is one of the smallest, although one of the oldest. This is my life now. I instruct seminarians at the monastery in the center of the city in the mornings and help look after the shrine here. You are welcome to come back. What is your name?"

"Keiji Hakagawa."

"Very good, Hakagawa san."

Keiji went back to the village. One day towards the end of the term he told the school administrator he would not be back for the next term. "I'm sorry to hear that. We do not have a lot of men in the country to do this."

"Yes, I know. I am sorry for you, but it is not my calling."

"What are you going to do, Hakagawa? What is your calling? Where are you going to go?" asked the principal.

"I am going to Kyoto. It is a holy place. Maybe I will find inspiration. Teaching science to 11-year olds is not for me. I have discovered that I am not a very good teacher, in the end. But I thank you for having me here."

"Young man, you have been an excellent teacher. It is just that many of these boys do not want to be taught. Their fathers are gone. No guidance. Little example to follow. This generation of children is rudderless. It is a bad omen for the future of Japan." The school principal hesitated a moment, then continued. "May you find happiness in what you do. We will get along here." The two men bowed. Keiji then turned and left the office.

In the meantime, Keiji had decided to explore becoming a priest. The more he thought about it, the better he felt.

Three weeks later, Kyoto......

"I am back. I have given my resignation to the school. The term ends in two weeks. I am ready to proceed on another path. I would like to consider becoming a priest. Could we talk about that? And, if I do become a priest, I would like to be associated with this shrine. My inspiration has come from it," said Keiji, as he sat with the priest.

"Very good. Military man to priest. It is not the usual path. But you appear to be sincere about it. Forgive me my doubts, Hakagawa san."

"I understand, but I have decided to pursue the priesthood. I want to do it."

"As to belonging here, you can belong to this shrine in time, but you must first receive the proper training."

"I understand. What do I do for it? Where do I go?" asked Keiji.

"There is the program of Shinto studies at the university in Ise, at Kokagakkan University. It is the most prestigious program in Japan. I recommend you apply for that. I can help you. Anyone who completes their studies for the priesthood at this university becomes a member of a priestly class above the rest in the country. I recommend you do the two-year program to qualify you as a Meikai, allowing you to be designated as a head priest." The priest paused a moment, then continued. "It is good you are doing this. We need priests. So many men died in the war. Because of that, we have had to accept women in the priesthood. It is not traditional. I will help you. You must make your application to the university now. Do it soon. I will sign it for you."

"Very good. Thank you."

"There is something else that must be spoken of. I notice you have an injured leg. You may have difficulty as a priest because of that. We priests sit in *seiza*, a position with our legs folded beneath us, often for long periods of time. You will have to be able to move into and out of this position with ease, and with dignity. You must be able to learn and do very complicated, demanding physical movements and you must do them in a dignified manner. It is necessary to have a high level of physical grace, balance and motor control. It may not seem important to you, but it is. You will have to be able to do it. I hope your condition will not disqualify you from this."

"I understand. I will have to work at it."

Chapter 9

San Diego, California, April 1946

Bob Kane walked into the lobby of the administration building of the sprawling military hospital campus.

"I am here to see Nurse Kathleen McLean. We knew each doing the war. She told me to check in here and ask you to advise her that I was here to see her."

"Nurse McLean. Let me see....." The woman at the desk looked into a three-ring binder on her desk. "Yes, she works in the ward next door. I will call over there. What is your name?"

"Robert Kane."

Twenty minutes later, Katie McLean walked into the lobby, saw Bob and walked over to him. It had been over four years since the two had seen each other. "Hello, Katie. Been a long time." An awkward moment followed. Bob didn't know what to do. As they looked at each other, he blurted out, "Can I give you a hug?"

"You sure can, Bob Kane." The two embraced. Bob pulled away and looked around. There were other people walking through the lobby.

"Can we find a corner or an office where we can talk? Pretty public here."

"Down the hall. There is a reception room. Follow me."

Bob closed the door to the room and turned to see Katie with a tear in her eye. He hugged her once again.

"I never thought I would see you again. But I thought of you all the time, Katie. I fell for you that day, before all hell broke loose. I wanted so much to see you again."

"I liked you too, Bob. So much happened after that. Seeing you in the hospital was strange. I thought you were dead. But it is so long ago, now."

"Yes, I know. So long ago." Bob hesitated a moment. He was not sure what to say, how far he should go. He decided to go for it, say what he wanted to say. "You must know that I have thought about you constantly, ever since that day. I loved you that day. I wanted to know if it was still there. I think it still is." He saw that Katie was uncomfortable, trying to read his intentions. He went on. "You should know that you saved my life that day."

"How do you mean, Bob…me saving your life?"

"I was thinking of you so much that morning, wide awake at 5AM, tossing and turning. I had to get up, do something. I did. Got up, got a cup of coffee in the galley, had breakfast and went on deck. If I hadn't met you and had just an ordinary time with the boys, I would have slept in like just about everybody else that Sunday morning, and I would be dead. You woke me up and saved me, Katie." Bob looked at her, trying to discern what feeling she had. He had laid it all out. "I have a big question for you. And I want you to tell me."

"What is it, Bob?"

"Can we pick up from where we left off that day?"

Katie McLean hesitated.

"I think we can. Maybe we can start. I've been through a lot. And, from your letter, so have you. I'm not saying no."

She crossed the floor and put her arms around Bob's neck, held on for a second, then leaned back, looking into Bob's eyes with their arms still around each other. "I've got a good idea for a start. The Tommy Dorsey orchestra is playing tonight at the Armed Forces complex downtown. They have a big dance floor for it. I'll get tickets somehow. Chattanooga Choo-Choo once again. How about it?"

"Yes, Katie. Chattanooga Choo-Choo once again....... and whatever other songs they play."

"In the meantime, I have to go. Need to get back to work. We can talk all we want later."

"Ok. Where do I meet you?"

"The nurse's dormitory is just down the campus road here. Fourth building over, going north. See you in the lobby at 6:30? We can grab a bite on the way. Ok?"

"Ok. See you at 6:30. Can I kiss you?"

"You sure can." Bob kissed Katie on the cheek, held her hands a moment in his, then left.

Later, after dancing to many of the tunes of the orchestra and the continuous banter with other couples at their table, Bob and Katie were seated in a lounge down the street from the concert bowl.

"You know, Katie, I have not had fun like this since that day before the attack. Also, I never thought I would see you again."

"Well, it's the same for me," replied Katie.

"But I ran into Irene. Thank God I did."

"Yes, it's a good thing you did. I'm glad you're here."

"Before running into Irene, long before that, I learned that you were married." He looked at Katie. She was listening, but said nothing. "Maybe this is not the time and maybe you don't want to talk about it, but tell me about your husband. If you want to. He must have been quite a guy."

"He was. Gentle, kind, fun. I loved him. But it's past. He's gone. I really enjoyed tonight." She continued to look at Bob. He did not know what to say. He wanted to ask her. He did not want to blow it. He held back. It was an awkward moment.

Katie was anticipating that Bob would ask the question.

"I'm sorry about your husband. Maybe we should talk about something else."

She sensed the hesitation. Maybe just as well. He just arrived. She broke the silence.

"The four years in between, Bob. What did you do? Your letter told me a bit, but what happened to you?"

"Got shipped to Seattle for full recovery, then decided I wanted to get back into it. Crazy, but I needed to do it. Couldn't just leave all of it and go back to whatever. There was not much to go back to. I applied for officer candidate school and got accepted. After graduation, I was given command of a landing craft for the invasions of the islands we needed to take back. I later became the commander of a whole squadron of them, then was part of the occupation force in Japan after the surrender. That's basically what the four years were about."

"How was all that? Want to talk about it?"

"I'll talk about it. Maybe help get it out of my system. What was it all about?......Heroism, sacrifice, slaughter, the best of America, so much of it lost - in the water, on the beaches, in the hills. The Japs. They never surrendered. Fought to the end, just like cornered animals. We had to kill them all. They say their honor prevented them from surrendering. Such a waste. Their men, our men. Saw many men die. Just like at Pearl that day. Had three of my crewmen die in my arms. The images, the memory, the smells of cordite, of burning flesh will stick with me, I'm afraid. I wake up at night. I hope it can go away, but I'm not sure."

"I saw much of it, too. All the broken men they shipped to us."

"Let's not talk about it anymore, Katie. At least not now. We've both had enough of it. It will take a long time for me to get over it. The Japs, the Japanese, I will never have anything to do with them. That is for sure."

"Yes, enough."

Bob wondered at that moment if he had blown the occasion.

"Let's talk about something else. When are you going home? Can I see you tomorrow, by the way?"

"Yes, you will. We'll do something else. We can go to the amusement park. The big roller coaster, it's huge, and there are other great rides as well. It's fun. I've been dying to go, but nobody asked me."

"And, about going home. Two months from now. That's the way it looks," said Katie. "Talking about something else, where is your family now? Were they in the war? Who do you have to go back to?" asked Katie.

"Well, there's not much left of it." Bob unfolded his family's story. After it, he hesitated a moment before continuing. "I have not seen my sisters for a long time. My family back home with who I interact is basically my aunt Barbara in Topeka. It's my base back home for the moment. My sisters are out in the country somewhere, on farms raising kids I am told, but I don't even know where anymore...... You know, there were so many guys like me who joined the navy, the army, for a better life. There was nothing for us in Kansas in the '30's. It hasn't been that long ago, although it seems like a lifetime. You know about that, I am sure. Military life was a release from those tough times. The hardships of war were not all that more difficult than what most of us had lived growing up. Shoot, I knew guys who received the first new pair of pants in their lives when they joined the navy. Enlisting gave us something to do. Then the war came......What about you, Katie? How did you get to that afternoon at Waikiki?"

"Ran away from home, basically. That, and the fact I always wanted to be a nurse. My dad lost his job in the depression and from being a relatively well-to-do family in the early '30's, we hit pretty near rock bottom. My mom was able to keep her teacher's job, but I had to get away. I saw an ad for the navy and nurse's training and jumped at it. I was eighteen. Ended up soon enough in Hawaii. A little paradise. Then it all went crazy. Mom and Dad are still alive. Actually doing fairly well now. Dad's back working and my mother is now a school principal. They seem happy once again and I will be seeing them in a few weeks."

The following Sunday afternoon on the beach..

"I can't stay here much longer, Katie. I have to go back to Topeka and I'm running out of money." He wanted to pop the ultimate question ever since he had arrived, but it would not come out.

Katie looked at Bob. "What are you going to do, in the end, Bob?"

Bob thought for a moment, then turned to her and blurted out, "Marry you."

She laughed. "It's about time, Bob Kane. I was wondering how long it would take. But what I meant was what you want to do - career, job, that."

"Don't laugh, Katie, damn it. I want to marry you. Will you marry me? The rest will come. I have wanted to get to this since the moment I arrived here. Will you marry me?"

"Yes, I will. I knew it would come to this when I saw you. It sure took you long enough."

"I had to get to know you," he said with a sheepish grin.

"Bull, Bob Kane, you had the idea all along. Yes, I will marry you." I am glad, she thought. I will do this. I hardly know him, but I will do this. She then turned, pushed Bob back onto the sand, stretched out over him and kissed him. "Are you happy?" she asked as she looked down at him.

"I am happy. Very happy."

They kissed again.

Later that evening, at a diner off the beach..

"This is all pretty quick. We hardly know each other," said Bob once they had taken their seats in the booth.

"I know. It is. Do you want to back out?" Katie had a frown on her face.

"No. I'm in love with you. I want to spend the rest of my life with you. I always have."

Bob hesitated a moment, looking at Katie, then reached across the table to take her hand. "It's a bit unreal. We have spent a total of something like sixteen hours together, for God's sake, including that day five years ago. But I don't want to back out. I ask you again, will you marry me, Katie McLean?"

"Yes, I will, Bob Kane. Come here." Bob rose up with Katie beckoning him to lean over the table. She put her arms around his neck and kissed him. "This may be quick, but I am fine with that. I want to marry you, Bob. Just don't back out on me. Please don't."

"I won't, Katie. You're my lady. For life."

They both sat down, aware of the looks of the other people in the diner. Somebody started to clap. The other people chimed in. Soon everybody was clapping, voicing their approval of the show of love.

"Well, this is a good start," said Bob with a big smile on his face. "Everybody cheering." Bob rose, bowed left, then right. "Thank you, thank you. She just told me again she would marry me!" Bob sat back down, with a shy look on his face, looking at Katie. They then burst out laughing and waved to the people who were still clapping.

Katie spoke first. "The quickness of it. The war did it to us. It's how it was, how it made us think. About life. About living. During those years, we never knew if we or who we knew would be alive the next day, the next week. It was live the day, tomorrow may not be there. It's a carry over. We know little else. A war romance it is, even when the war is over. But, you know, I don't care. This is now. This is what I want to do. I believe in you, Bob Kane. I liked you when I first met you. Right away. I remembered the feeling the other day before you got here. You deserve to be loved. I'm getting there. Really. I am very happy marrying you. Can you love me?"

"I already do. I've loved you since December 6, 1941."

Bob leaned across the table and kissed Katie on the cheek. She drew him to her, and kissed him on the lips. "Let's celebrate this. Take me to your room, Bob." Spending the night with Katie was something that Bob had dreamt of for a long, long time. Over four years. It was finally happening.

"Where are we going to live? Topeka, somewhere else? Why not Hawaii? Beautiful. We could live there. The war is over." The two of them were in bed the next morning.

"Not Hawaii, Katie. Please. Never. I never want to go there again, nor even hear about it. Too much pain to relive. Too many Japanese people. We will live somewhere else."

"OK. Understand about Hawaii. Your ship, the attack."

"Katie, really. We can't talk about Hawaii, that day, the ship, any of that. It brings back too much pain." He hesitated, before continuing. "You know, I was part of the occupation force at the end in Japan. I almost killed people. People, citizens, not even soldiers, who I was responsible for looking after. I just wanted to obliterate them. I'm not like that. I realized the war had turned me into something else. I wasn't me anymore. I had to get out. I was supposed to be there for another four months, but I couldn't stand it. I never want to go back to Hawaii and certainly never back to Japan."

"What will you do now? For a living. Important question, future husband. You mentioned something about insurance the other day."

"Yes, it could be insurance, but it may be going back to college if I can wing it. I have a meeting with an insurance company in Omaha when I get back. An uncle in the business who helped me out with college before the war put me in touch with them. I may have a job with them in Kansas City, in sales, although I don't know anyone there. I may be able to finish college at the same time. Spread it out over four or five years. But I have to start somewhere and earn some income if we are going to be married. I'll need to support you."

"I will pull my share, my dear. I'm a nurse. There will always be a need for nurses, no matter where it is. Finishing college will be important for you, for us. I'm glad you are thinking about that. We'll make it, whatever we end up doing."

Bob and Katie were married in St. Louis, her hometown, three months later.

As a condition of marriage, Katie was never to mention to anyone that Bob was a survivor of the Arizona. The guilt he felt about surviving while his buddies died had not left him. Any reference to the war, if mentioned at all or if they were asked, was to start and end with Bob's service landing troops in the Pacific.

Bob was hired by the Iowa Mutual Life Insurance Company. He would be attached to the Kansas City office. Part of the agreement with the company was that he could attend college in the mornings and work the afternoons and evenings meeting prospects. He enrolled at Missouri State University in business administration, continuing what he had started at the university in Topeka three years before the war.

They moved into a rented house in a quiet neighborhood not far from his office and the university campus across the river.

Katie quickly found a job as an emergency ward nurse at the city's largest hospital. They began their life together.

One year later, their first child, a boy, was born. His name was John. Aunt Barbara in Topeka would say later the boy looked just like his uncle.

Chapter 10

October 1950

Bob opened the letter, forwarded to him from his aunt's address. The return address was one in Knoxville, Tennessee. Opening it, he quickly looked at the last page. Signed Davey…..Davey Poole. My God. He had not heard from his buddy since the war. No response to the letter he had sent after coming home, no response to another one sent to the VA hospital six months later, when he told him he had found Katie and married her. He did not even know where he was. Through a call to the hospital a few months earlier Bob had learned that David Poole was no longer a patient there and had no forwarding address to give. The receptionist suggested he contact the Veterans Administration in Washington. He opened the letter.

Dear Bob,

It has been a long time and I hope this gets to you. Your old Topeka address is the only one I have. I hope you are well and happy with your lovely Katie. I remember her. I could barely see at the time, my sight had not fully recovered, but I remember her from the hospital. What a girl, as I remember it. Just based on that, I tell you you are a lucky guy.

Yes, I got your letters. I was not ready to write back. I was not in good shape. At my lowest. I was in the VA in Memphis. It had been over four years since Pearl. I wanted to die and really came close to killing myself. I was petrified of going out, having people seeing my freak face, my mangled hands and all. I couldn't play my music anymore. My fingers were too damaged. The VA people said I could leave at the time, just the same, but I didn't. I didn't know what to do. Then your first letter came. As I look back on it, it saved me from killing myself. Thank you, Bob. What you said made me begin to realize I still had a life to live, but I was petrified of the world outside. I went back to your letter, read it again, and again. Your description of all those guys who died on the beaches, in the hills and caves of those islands, and that we were still alive and had a life to live made me realize that yes, I still had a life to live and perhaps there was a reason for me being saved. Then I got your second letter. Even though you were not even sure I was still around, you exhorted me again to look at life as a gift and do something. Well, I did. I applied to college, to the University of Tennessee. In engineering. I always wanted to build things. I didn't think I would be accepted, but I was. High school grades helped. I started in September three years ago, thanks to the GI Bill and a letter from my high school principal, with freak face and all. That's where I am now. My last year and already have a job offer starting next summer. Thank you, Bob. You saved my life. I will be forever indebted to you. I mean that. May we stay in touch. I promise I will be more responsive. Here's my phone number here. Your buddy, Davey.

Bob immediately placed a call to the number. There was no answer, but he called again that evening. Davey answered.

"Davey, this is Bob. Bob Kane. Got your letter today. Super. So glad to hear from you, old buddy."

"Good Lord, Bob. Yes. So glad to hear from you."

"I was worried about you, buddy" replied Bob. "Thought you may be dead. But you're not. Thank God."

"Yes, it has been a long time. I'm not dead, but lots of water has flowed under the bridge.....How are YOU?"

"I'm fine. Very happy. With my lady Katie and our two boys; John, who is three now and little David who was born a year ago. Making my way. Selling insurance and finishing college at the same time. Just about done with that."

"Bob, great. So great.....I meant it in the letter when I said you saved my life. You gave me the push I needed."

"Glad to hear that, Davey."

"Thank you, old friend, but it took me a while to accept what you laid on me."

"You know, that letter to you was written the same day as a letter to Katie, four years after I had last seen her as well. They were letters of hope. Changed lives in the end, both of them, it looks like. One that you say changed yours, and the other changing mine. Two letters written the same day. Hallelujah. God is somewhere after all."

"Yes, hallelujah. God is with us."

"You're right. Just like that day, but you know, Davey, I can't talk about it to anyone. It's too much."

"Well, you should talk about it. I talk about it. Not to everyone, but to a few. Some of the people around me. One is a psychologist. He's helped me get out of the darkness. Boy, was it dark."

"I know. I saw you" said Bob.

"It lasted a good while. I don't have nightmares as often anymore. Happens occasionally, but nowhere near as bad as the early days. Do you?"

"Yes, I do. Only Katie knows about my time on our ship. My family in Topeka, what's left of it anyway, doesn't talk about it. I asked them not to and they respect that - but the nightmares come and I wake up in a sweat. You know what it is. The fire, the explosions, the guys burning alive, I still can't handle it, so many not getting out. They're still down there, you know. Why those guys and not me."

"Bob, go see somebody to talk to. The VA. They have staff for that. You don't have to tie yourself up with this."

"Maybe I should. I've never wanted to or accept that I need to." Bob paused. There was silence on the line. "Let's talk about something else, Davey. The job you're going to. Tell me about it."

"Bob, listen. I'll be glad to talk about the job and all that, but I'm serious. The nightmares and the guilt stuff. Come on, man. Don't let it fester. Take care of it. Go to the VA. Tell them. Do it! I still feel guilty about surviving that day and I may never get that totally out of my system but I've learned to live with it. Don't let this drag you down, man."

"Ok. Maybe I will," Bob replied.

Bob and Davey would speak to each other regularly from that point forward, but Bob Kane would never manage to open up with anyone else about December 7 1941 and the USS Arizona until later in life. Much later.

Chapter 11

Summer 1953

"Daddy, look what I found. A sword. A real sword."

"No! No! No.! Give me that." Bob yelled at his son. "Where did you get that?" He was horrified. The sword he had taken off a dead Japanese officer at Okinawa. He had forgotten he had it.

"Upstairs, in the attic.. The door was open, so I went up. I was always scared to go up there, but all there is up there is a bunch of boxes, and I found the sword behind one of them."

"Give me the sword, son. This is not something to play with. Go on outside. Find your friend, Donnie."

Bob Kane then proceeded to the basement and broke the sword in two over an anvil. Katie had followed him and observed the destruction of the Japanese officer's sword.

"You're still fighting the Japs, Bob. You have to get over it."

"No souvenirs, Katie. I am not still fighting the Japs. I have been trying for years to forget it all. This brought it back. I want nothing to do with Japan, the Japanese, or anything from them. I had forgotten I still had the damn thing."

By that time, Bob Kane was established in the insurance business and building a successful career. He would stay in insurance for another twenty years, rising to the position of general agent for Kansas, Nebraska and Oklahoma for his company. He spoke at conventions and training sessions where his talent for motivating salespeople was recognized. At the age of 45, he resigned from the company and set up his own insurance brokerage, which grew rapidly. Within five years it had become one of the fastest growing brokerages in Eastern Kansas. Being his own boss also allowed him the opportunity to continue his motivational speaking, but for his own account. He wrote two books on selling in the three years after leaving the company. He was busy, which suited him. People did not know of his dark side. No one knew he was a survivor of the Arizona and he wanted to keep it that way.

During all the years following the war, Bob harbored a lingering hatred of the Japanese. He refused to go to Hawaii, even when company conventions were held there. He begged off as being sick or for other reasons. He believed the fate of his buddies was determined by the activities of spies of Japanese descent who claimed to be Americans in Hawaii.

Through Davey Poole, Bob was contacted by an Arizona survivors group that had formed an association, but he refused to join and told the people contacting him to stop trying to get him into it. The thought of that day in 1941 and the loss of his friends was hell. Later, in 1962, he became aware of the memorial that had been constructed over the remains of the ship in the harbor. He was determined to never go there.

In the meantime, Katie had trouble with all this. It was a difficult life for her in the periods of Bob's recurring problems with the memory of December 7. For long periods, he was immersed in his business and career, concealing his distress, managing to keep the thoughts of that day out of his mind. On the outside, he was a motivator, a successful guy, a writer about success and how to achieve it, but inside, not far from the surface of his everyday life, he was a festering mess. Despite the veneer of positive thinking, he was often 'not there.' At other times, and what saved their marriage, he was all there, a loving husband and father, devoted to Katie and their boys. But Katie never knew when the nightmares would return, triggering bouts of depression that would consume Bob for days at a time.

Katie implored him to seek help. Despite that and the suggestions from Davey Poole, he resisted it. He could not bear the thought of discussing it with anyone.

Chapter 12

Kyoto, Japan, September 1954

Keiji Hakagawa had completed his studies to be a Shinto priest in 1950. His rank of Meikai, given according to his exam results, qualified him to serve as a head priest, or Guji, at most shrines in Japan. He was the Guji at a shrine on the outskirts of Kyoto.

"I am happy with what I am doing. It allows me to help people, with their being, their soul, their purpose in life." Keiji was with an old friend, a fellow flight instructor from the war, now working as an engineer with a large company and visiting Kyoto, renewing contact with his old friend. "I am close to my family. My two daughters are growing quickly. They will be fine young ladies. I am at peace."

"Not like during the war, Keiji."

"No, not like during the war. I was not at peace then. I was actually horrified at what we were doing. We have never spoken of this."

"We have never spoken about it, but I saw things in you that were strange. Not part of a military mind. I did not think much of it. You were such a good instructor. The attack of Pearl Harbor. You were involved, yes?"

"Yes, I was involved. I commanded a squadron of Kates. We bombed the American battleships, one in particular. I was appalled. It has never left me. It drove me to this life."

"What is the life. Keiji?"

"Allowing and encouraging our people to respect and protect our spiritual and cultural heritage. It is strong. It is what makes us who we are as Japanese and able to live in harmony with nature. I help protect the conscience of our society. An everyday devotion to it."

"And it satisfies you? We were warriors, Keiji. I had no idea you would ever go to something like this."

"I was not a warrior. I hid it. I have peace now. It is my calling."

Chapter 13

October 1964

"Dad, the Olympics are starting. There are guys from Kansas in it."

Bob heard his son, but he was not interested. The games. In Tokyo. The hell with them. The hell with Japan.

"You go ahead, John. I've got things to do." Bob Kane would not be watching any of it.

"You're still going too far on this, Bob. The war ended twenty years ago," said Katie after their 17-year old son had left the kitchen.

"I don't care. I'm not going to watch anything coming from Japan."

"That's why you find a reason to not go to those conventions and company getaways in Hawaii. You overdo it. Can't you get over this?"

"Quiet, Katie. Quiet. I won't hear about it."

A few days later..

"Dad, remember when I was little and I found a sword? The one I found in the attic?"

"Yes, I remember."

"It was a Japanese sword, wasn't it? From the war."

"What about it, John? You will know I destroyed that sword that day. I was in the war. I forgot I had it and I didn't want it around anymore."

"I know. And I remember. You were pretty mad. You yelled. I never heard you yell so loud. Never saw you like that again."

"Well, the war was difficult. Very difficult. I saw many men die. I don't like to be reminded of it."

"Is that where you got the stuff on your arms?" The scars on Bob's arms had faded but they were still there. The boys had never asked him about them.

No, not going there. "No, that happened on the farm when I was 16. A barn fire. We put it out but my arms got burned a bit."

"What did you do in the war, Dad?"

"Do we have to talk about that, son? I have been trying to keep it out of my mind ever since."

"You were in the navy. Why don't you want to tell us? It's about you, our dad. Please, Dad. It's about you and your life. We want to know more about it. It's a gap we know nothing about. Where were you in the war? Were you at Pearl Harbor? Aunt Barbara told me a couple years ago our uncle John was killed there. What about you? Were you there?"

"I was not at Pearl when that happened. I was on my way to officer school. I landed troops on islands. For four years. I saw many men die and I don't want to talk about it, John."

"Mom won't tell us either. She was in Hawaii during the war but when it comes to you, it's all vague. It's too bad, Dad. There is a lot about you we just don't know. I wish you would tell us more."

Later, in the middle of the night, Bob bolted up in bed, screaming "Fire, Fire, Billy, Billy!" Katie awoke, rose up and turned to Bob, still half asleep, but shaking, with his hands covering his face. He turned to Katie, who had turned on the light. "I couldn't save anybody, Katie. I was in the water, a plane coming at me, shooting, the splashes coming at me, the guy next to me, rounds hitting him, throwing him up and out of the water like a doll, then flat, looking up with half his face gone."

"Bob, you have to end this."

Bob continued. "I was crying, bawling, shaking as I tried to swim. Guys screaming, yelling, the smell of burning flesh, a guy's head on fire, he was screaming, yelling, 'Momma save me. Momma where are you?' I knew him. He was 18 and he was on fire. I couldn't save him."

"Bob, you have to see somebody about this. I implore you."

"I know. I know, Katie. I'm sorry."

November, 1968

"Dad, this is not right. We have no business being in Vietnam. The people there should be left to work it out themselves. We have no business there. It's all wrong. John could be going there, could be killed and for what?"

David Kane was nineteen and part of an anti-war group at his college in Iowa. He was home for the Thanksgiving holiday and the war was the topic of discussion.

"America has to go to war from time to time. Defend what we are about, David."

"This is madness. The youth of the country are rising up against it. We are slaughtering people over there and wasting young American lives doing it. I won't go if I get drafted, Dad. I won't. I'll go to Canada. John will surely be sent. He has no exemption any more. How did this happen? That he could go?"

"You know what his situation is. He has graduated. He could be drafted now. He is enlisting in the Air Force to avoid being drafted into the army. With his degree in engineering, he will probably be in a technical position. He won't be infantry and he won't be a fighter pilot. If he goes to Vietnam, it will most surely not be in the front line. He can serve his country just the same. You get called to serve your country. It's part of being American."

"Dad, that's bullshit. This war is not just. You were in a war that was justified. This one's not."

"Don't talk to me about my war, David."

"Why not, Dad? You seem to justify this war because you were in one twenty five years ago. Why don't you want to talk about it? What did you go through? Did you kill?"

"David, you have no idea what I went through and I don't want to talk about it."

"But if it was so bad, as it seems, why are you so silent about this war that could cost you your own son?" David then got up from the table, grabbed his jacket and went out the front door.

Katie had been listening from the living room. She got up, found her way to the dining room and said to Bob "Bob, you have to confront this with your sons. You should tell them about what you went through. They should know that. David believes you to be indifferent about this war, this war that is tormenting the young men of the country, including him. They should know just how much you have wanted to forget everything about war, that you are against war, and why. You went through it. The killing. The devastation. And David is right. If what you went through was so bad, why would you not do everything you could to oppose war and spare young lives, just like the many, many young lives of our generation who lost their lives in the one that we knew?"

"Katie, I am not in favor of war."

"Then why don't you do something about it? You are a speaker. People look up to you. You have an audience. One of your sons is about to be put in jeopardy for an unjust war, and the second one could become a draft dodger and be exiled from his country and from us because of it. This war is close to home, Bob. It is not a patriotic war like the one you were in. It is something else, and you have the power to do something about it."

"No, I don't Katie. You're going too far. I can't use my speaking business to come out against the war, against our government."

"You are letting your patriotism take precedence over reason and over our own good, as a family, and as a country as well. Are you for this war on the other side of the world or are you against it, Bob? Tell me, which is it? I can't believe you would be for it after all you went through. And if you are against it, you should do something about it. Our sons deserve that. If the fathers and mothers of the country rose up in protest like our youth are doing, maybe the people in Washington will put an end to this. In the meantime, our boys are in danger and for something that is crazy."

"Katie, you are making this very difficult for me."

"You owe it to your sons."

Bob got up from the table, put his coat on and said as he walked out the door. "I'm going for a walk."

"You'll probably see David on the way."

"So be it."

"Just hug him, Bob. Hug him."

One year later...

Dear Mom and Dad, I'm here now, but can't say where it is. A base. I'm in charge of runway maintenance. There is action not that far away, but we are safe. The perimeter is pretty secure. There is devastation around us, though. I wish I could say we are right being here. It's more complicated than that. I can't say any more.

Love you all. I am well. Don't worry about me. I brush my teeth every day, Mom. All the best. Love, John.

Katie put down the letter and cried. Earlier that day, she had received a call from Air Force Command in Colorado Springs. Their son, John, had been wounded. He had been shot in the back during an intrusion at the base where he was stationed. They would be able to see him at a military hospital just outside of Sacramento, where he was being transferred.

She had placed the call to the hotel in Minneapolis soon after and left the message on his room phone. "Bob, John has been shot. He's on his way to a hospital in California. I knew it would come to this! Call me." Katie was crying.

An hour later, Bob was on the phone. "What? What happened? Shot? How? He was not supposed to be near the action."

"We got a letter from him today in the mail. Sent before he was shot. He said he was at a base with a secure perimeter. He was in charge of runway maintenance. I have no idea of what happened. Bob, come home. We're going to California."

"Yes. I'm going to the airport. I'll call you to let you know when I arrive. Where is he?"

"Near Sacramento. The caller gave me the address of the hospital."

"OK. I will book a flight for us when I get to the airport."

"I knew it would come to this. You were so permitting of this, Bob. Patriotic duty. So much bullshit! My son, our son. You let it happen!"

"Katie, you are not right about that."

"Part of being American. It's all wrong, Bob Kane. You and I saw too much of this to let it happen again."

"Katie, I'm coming home. I'm sorry. We will go see John."

Airman 1st Class John Kane was asleep when Bob and Katie arrived. "He is sedated. He is being operated on this evening," said the nurse who accompanied the parents to their son's room. Katie approached the bed and took her son's hand.

"What is his condition? He was hit in the back, we are told," asked Bob of the nurse as Katie stroked her son's hand.

"You will have to speak to the doctor, Mr. Kane. I can try to track him down. I believe he is here this afternoon."

"Your son took a bullet in the spine. He is paralyzed at this time, from the neck down," said the neurosurgeon. "We are operating this evening to extract the bullet and relieve pressure on the spine. There is no time to lose. It has already been 72 hours since he was hit. We must relieve the pressure and see what we can do to restore feeling and mobility."

"Is it permanent?" asked Katie.

"It may be, Mrs. Kane. The prognosis is not good right now. I'm sorry to have to tell you that. We will know more tonight."

"He looks like nothing happened to him."

"I don't know the circumstances. All I can tell you is that he took a bullet in the back. He was not shot anywhere else," responded the doctor.

Bob then spoke up. "I am former military. I was in the Pacific theatre. My wife is a nurse and was in the military in the war as well. Who could we speak to who would know what happened?"

"Speak to the administrator, Mr. Kane. His office is on the ground floor. They may be able to connect you to someone with knowledge of what happened. Hopefully, the information you are seeking is not classified. In the meantime, Sir, we will try to minimize the long-term damage to your son, but I must tell you that he may be paralyzed, from where to where, we don't know yet."

"Can we speak to him before the operation?"

"I'm afraid not. We are trying to keep him totally immobile. Asleep, basically. I'm sorry."

"Thank you, doctor."

"We don't know exactly what happened, Mr. Kane," explained the deputy director of the hospital. "All we have on file is that he was stationed at an airbase near Saigon and was shot in the back, obviously during an attack on the base or his living quarters, an incursion of some sort. Getting the details of that could prove to be difficult for you. You would have to speak to someone in the chain of command at the base. That could take time. You may end up having to rely on what your son tells you when he can. What did the doctor say about his condition?"

"He is operating on our son this evening. A few hours from now. We'll see how he comes out of it. Can we come back later? See our son after the operation?"

"You could try, but you may be restricted. Visiting hours end at 9. Probably be best to come back tomorrow morning."

As Bob and Katie walked through the front door, he saw an ambulance parked at the far entrance to the hospital. A stretcher was being taken out of the van. Two orderlies were preparing to retrieve other stretchers laden with wounded men.

"This is just like then, Katie. It's no different."

"Boys. Boys being destroyed. We can't let this happen anymore."

"Let's get out of here. I can't take this."

"Bob, we can't let this continue. No more. No more. I will not have it. One son possibly destroyed is enough. No more. We must do something."

"I'm sorry. I'm afraid it is permanent," said the doctor the following morning. "From the waste down, to be sure. He should have use of his arms, however, but he will most likely never walk again. I'm sorry."

"No. Please." Katie had tears in her eyes. The doctor continued. "The VA will be able to provide him therapy, maybe get him some use of his legs over time. It may be possible. The spinal cord was not completely severed in the lower back where he was hit. I would like to think I am not giving you false hope. It will be difficult. You must accept that."

"Thank you, doctor. I understand. Can we see him now?"

"Yes, you can. He should be awake. I saw him earlier. He knows he is paralyzed. He told me. I didn't have to tell him. He couldn't feel his legs. I said that therapy could help. I tried to give him hope."

"Hi, Mom. Hi Dad." Tears came to his eyes. "I can't walk, Dad. I can't feel my legs." Tears rolled down his face. "What am I going to do? What am I going to do with my life now?"

"John, you are going to make the best of it. It happened. Your life is not over. You will have your arms and hands, your head. It is all still there. It's not over."

"Dad, I will never walk again! I know it! No family, no children. No fishing and hunting again. Ever. Shooting baskets...or anything else! I will be in a fucking wheelchair forever!"

"You may not be. The doctor says you could have therapy, maybe walk again."

"Bullshit, Dad. It's bullshit. I'm paralyzed, for Christ's sake!"

"Hey, brother. I'm here. Lookin' after you for a few days." David had come home from college. It was spring break. John had arrived two days before from California. He would be at home after spending three months in the hospital, with extensive out-patient access to the VA hospital sixty miles away. Katie had insisted upon him being at home. She would look after him.

"Great, Dave. Good to see you, man. Sorry I can't take you one on one any more, though." John was trying to smile, to laugh, but it was not coming out easily.

"We'll find something else. Cards. Bets on football. It will be something." David had difficulty hiding his reaction to his brother's condition. He had been told John had lost thirty pounds, but he was still surprised. His brother had shrunk. "What happened, bro? You weren't supposed to be close to live fire."

"I'll tell you. But you have to promise me something, David. You won't go there. Do whatever you can to stay in school, extend your deferment. It's crazy, us being over there."

"You don't have to tell me about that. Mom and Dad have probably told you about my activity concerning the war."

"A bit. Mom said you got arrested by campus police last month."

"Yeah. Led a march protesting a general who was speaking on the war and why we needed to be there. No real big deal, but I'm not going to stop."

"Just don't get yourself drafted."

"If I do, I'm going to Canada. Drives Mom crazy, but I would do it. No way I'm going over there."

"Four or five months ago, I would have been upset if you told me that. Not now. Look at me. Nothing over there can justify what the war has done to me. What is it now - 40,000 of our guys dead so far? - that the government will not admit to. How many others that are like me in wheelchairs, with their heads messed up. I was doing my duty. What bullshit. We have no business being there."

"What happened? How did you get shot? Dad told me you were in charge of a runway for supply planes, in a secure area."

"Nothing is secure over there, David. It was early morning. Just after dawn. I was to make sure nothing was on the main runway; there was a bunch of planes loaded with stuff that was scheduled to come in that morning. As I rounded the corner of the hangar, shots were being fired. I could see them as they came through an opening in the fence. I have no idea how they breached it. The viet guys were supposed to prevent that. I turned around to go back but I didn't make it to the corner of the building. I got hit. I blacked out. Hit in the back. Lower part, just back here. One bullet. That's all it took....all it took to get me this way. God damn it. God damn it all......David, you go and protest. You raise hell. Raise absolute hell with this war." John looked out the window to the front yard. David saw that his brother's eyes had watered up. He started to speak again, while continuing to gaze out the window. "You remember Dougie Barnes, my buddy from high school, Dave?"

"Yeah, I do. I remember him. What about him?"

"He was there. I ran into him in Saigon a few days before the attack on the base. On the street. I was there for a free weekend. Complete surprise. Hardly recognized him. Piercing eyes, face like leather, beard, shaved head. He was always clean cut before, hair combed just right. Not like that anymore. He flagged me down. Came and grabbed my arm in a crowd. We went and had a beer. Said he had been in 'Nam for close to a year. Infantry. Special operations. Led a platoon in the central highlands, rooting out vc's. But spaced out...wow. Said he had kids under his command who died in his arms. Guys eighteen, nineteen years old. Said he couldn't take it anymore. He had always been mild-mannered, a gentle person. But he told me he had become a killer. The guy I was with that afternoon was not the guy I knew. He was on to weed. Couldn't sleep right. A mess...Scary what this war is doing to guys.....Dave, keep doing what you're doing. Just stay away from getting dragged over there."

"I have no intention of letting that happen. What are you going to do now? What do they tell you?"

"Therapy. Have to go to the VA in Topeka for that. Doctor back in California said I may be able to get back some use of my legs. I don't see it. I have no feeling in them. Mom says she'll take me to Topeka however many times it will take - twice a week, three times a week. Whatever. I don't know about the rest. Graduate school. Not likely. I've got an engineering degree. Master's in engineering. Right. I don't think so. Dad says I should apply to law school. Become a lawyer. Yeah... plead cases in a wheelchair. I don't know, David. But I can't just do nothing."

"I feel for you, man. Really do. Let's have a beer."

Later that evening..

David walked into the living room and saw his dad, sitting alone, staring out the big window facing the street. He gave no indication he recognized his son's presence. David went to the side of the chair where his father was sitting, and touched his shoulder. "Dad, you OK?"

His father continued to look out the window. A few seconds passed. Nothing. He then said. "Not really, David. I can't take this, seeing him this way. I can't take it." David could see that his father was choking up. Bob then turned to his son. "What can I do, what should I do, son? This is about you as well as about your brother. Your generation. All of this. Slaughter, coffins, body bags, wheel chairs. What do you think I should do?" David was taken aback. It was the first time his father had ever asked him for advice.

It did not take long for David to respond. He had had an idea in his mind for awhile. Now was the time to speak of it. "You address audiences, Dad. You seem to reach people. How about reaching people about this? What I mean is reaching your generation, parents, the people in power. Reach them, shake them, Dad. Our generation is being wasted in the jungle and hills halfway around the globe for nothing. You could do it, Dad."

"Your mother tells me the same thing. Ganging up on me, huh?"

"Mom and I have not spoken about this. That it comes from us independently should tell you something, however. You could use what you already have, Dad. In abundance, for God's sake. If you wanted to."

"Maybe I will." Bob looked at his son. "Maybe I will. Let's go see John. He's in the TV room."

David Kane returned to his college in Iowa a few days later. He was involved in organizing a big demonstration to be held in Des Moines in April. The Secretary of Defence was to give a speech regarding the war and America'a defense capability. The students were determined to disrupt it.

Bob Kane was on the phone. "David, that demonstration you told me about when you were here. The one you are organizing. Des Moines, right? When is it again?"

"Yes, Dad. Des Moines. April 20. Friday. Last day of classes on Thursday before exams. Why?"

"I'll be there."

Three weeks later, after the demonstration had ended and the crowds had dispersed, Bob sat with David in a roadside cafe. The place was packed with truckers, with their rigs lined up in the parking lot.

"You sure you're OK, David? That's quite a bump on your head." David Kane's jacket was torn at the shoulder and there was mud on the sleeve.

"I'm Ok, Dad. The policeman hit me pretty good, but I got away. A bunch of others did not. I'm glad you found me."

"All I had to do was find the front of the crowd. You were there, flailing away. Placards and all. Leading the way. Doing a good job of it. Mom will probably be able to repair your jacket, by the way."

"I hope I don't get expelled. I could be drafted if that happens. But I gotta do it, Dad. Have to continue."

"You won't be expelled. I heard your chancellor on the radio this morning before the demonstration as I was driving in. He was saying the students had a right to protest. 'It's their war and their lives, in the end,' he said, mentioning as well that the demonstration had been OK'd by the Des Moines authorities."

"Well, well, the old man is coming around. He wasn't this way last year or even in the fall. Had campus police get after us every time we tried something. I'm still not sure about not being expelled." David looked at his Dad. "What did you think? Did we not raise some hell?"

"Yes, you did. But I don't think you will be expelled. It was the police who turned things ugly."

"Well, what about you?"

"I'm doing it, David. Speaking about it. Mobilizing. I'm working on a plan with some people."

"How, Dad? How are you going to do it? Come right out and speak? Publicly?"

"Yep. You and Mom are right. I do this already. Why not do it for a cause? I found a parents-against-the war organization in St. Louis and another one in Chicago. I have spoken to both groups. They're getting bigger every day. One of them has as many uncles and aunts in it as parents. I told them what I did for a living. They're enthused. We're organizing a big public meeting for Chicago in mid-June. We'll get media there, everything. A couple of the parents are in the media, network television apparently. They have to be careful, but have assured us there will be coverage."

"I'm sure there will be, Dad. Parents protesting. Not just hippies, privileged college kids and draft-dodgers anymore."

"We are setting up other meetings in Denver and San Francisco in May and Boston later in June. Got lots of people helping,"

Suddenly, one of the truckers at the next table who had overheard Bob and David's conversation, turned around, got up, took two steps over and pounded his fist on the table, leaning into David's face. "Fucking anti-war demonstrator, huh? This your old man here? I oughta kick both of your asses. My buddies here I am sure would help. We don't need people like you. Unpatriotic sons-of-bitches."

Bob Kane got up and swung hard. He caught the man flush on the jaw, knocking him to the floor. "Nobody will ever call me unpatriotic. If you want to fight, we're on, buddy. Right there, outside," as he looked over the man, writhing on the floor. The man's friends rose from their table, started to advance hesitantly toward Bob, but stopped. The owner of the diner, a big man, had not been far away and quickly got between the two tables. "I'll have to ask you all to leave. Pay your bills and leave or I'm calling the fuzz. Out." The diner was packed. Everyone had stopped talking and were watching. "Let's get out of here, David." Bob put a twenty dollar bill on the table, grabbed David's arm and moved to the door. Everyone in the diner watched them as they left. The truckers followed, looking menacingly at Bob and David as they crossed the parking lot, but said nothing.

"Dad, you knocked him cold. I never saw you do anything like that. Amazing." David was trying to keep up with his dad as angrily and briskly walked to the car.

"War can do that to you, son. Got into a few fights at your age. But don't ask me to talk about it."

Two weeks later, at Kent State University in Ohio, National Guardsmen opened fire on demonstrating students. Four students were shot dead.

Bob Kane was on his way to being a Vietnam war protester.

Chapter 14

Eight months later, February 6, 1971, 6:45 PM, CBS Evening News, WBBM Chicago

"Mr. Kane, through the Parents-Against-the-War organization, you are galvanizing opposition to the war. Demonstrations are occurring across the nation, not by young people, but by middle-aged, mainstream Americans. There was one today in Chicago. People are watching this, and I am sure the President is as well. It looks to be feeding a groundswell of opposition."

"Yes, very much so, a tide of voices of opposition from concerned parents, aunts, uncles, grandfathers and grandmothers. We simply have to stop this, Jane. It has been a terrible mistake, costing us thousands of our youth. Nothing justifies it."

"You repeat this in all your statements. You are certainly consistent."

"Yes, I believe I am. We have to stop it. It has been a terrible mistake. Nothing justifies it. We have to end it. A good advocate for something will tell his audience what he is going to say, will say it, then tell the audience what he has just said. I follow that credo, and maybe it is annoying to many, but my message and the message of all those people active in this movement, is the same everywhere. The parents of this American generation deserve a mouthpiece, if you will, maybe even a bull horn. I am happy to be that bull horn. I have a son crippled by the war. I don't want a second one lost or crippled by it. That goes as well for every other young American out there. As a nation, as a people, we cannot afford to lose one more of our young men. This war is a mistake and it has to end."

Three days later..

The telephone rang. Bob answered while looking at his watch…9:30 pm. Who could be calling at this hour?

"Hello."

"Is this Robert Kane?" Bob did not recognize the voice.

"Yes, it is. Who is calling?"

"Never mind who's calling. You are a damn traitor. I hope you burn in hell, you sonofabitch. Continue what you're doing, Kane, and you will die, and it will be good riddance." Before Bob had a chance to say anything, the man hung up. The next day, Bob had the Kane home phone number changed to an unlisted number. Only close friends, family and key associates in Parents Against the War were given the new number.

Chapter 15

June 1971

Headline: Congress Votes to Bring Troops Home.

After putting the paper down, Davey called his old buddy. "You've really done it, Bob. You're in the news all the time. That big march on Washington. You got it done. Congress telling the president to end this. Bring the troops home by year's end. He's getting the message."

"I never thought we, in particular me, would ever do something to oppose our government," replied Bob. "Never thought I would, man."

"He's got to do it now," said Davey. "The draft has ended. At least no more of our kids will be sent into it against their will. I don't have any, but we are all fathers to the kids over there. You gotta be proud, old buddy."

"My boys brought me to it. Katie as well. And I'm glad they did. It has not been without trouble, though."

"I thought you were crazy last year, when you started. I was not in favor then. But I am now. Stupid war. Such a waste.

You've done it, buddy. Parents-Against-the-War. I'm seeing it all over. TV. The papers."

"It's not over yet, Davey. We still have a long way to go. There are 400,000 men still over there, some getting killed every day. We're not letting up just because of the votes in Congress. We're still mobilizing. We have to keep it up."

"You must get a lot of pushback. Lots of folks don't like what you're doing."

"That's for sure. Get it all the time. We've been treated as radicals, in cahoots with revolutionaries, friends of anarchists. Misguided delusionists was a term I saw recently. Communists. All sorts of stuff, Davey. I'm fortunate enough to be solid financially. But there are people out there who would love to ruin me. Despite them, we are on the right side of this and we are winning."

"How are your boys, by the way?" asked Davey.

"John is trying to make the best of life. But he's weak. He's vulnerable. He's taking a course in law by correspondence, but he's not really into it. I worry about him. Katie dotes on him. I don't know what the future lies for him. David, who I named after you, by the way, although he doesn't know it because I would have to tell him and his brother about Pearl, is graduating next year from college. Wants to go to grad school. Our chief demonstrator. Quite committed. He will be fine. Looks after his brother all he can."

"What really did it for you? I mean to go this far? Your son is paying the price, I know, but you are really out there."

"What did it for me to begin with was certainly the ruining of the life of my son – he is not getting over anything - and the impact it has had on Katie. What pushed me further were the young veterans who came to us and told us their stories. Broken men who wanted and needed to talk. They told us the U.S. could not possibly win the war. No way. Killing people for nothing. We had to end it. It was very compelling. I knew I had to take it further. Now, hundreds of thousands of Americans have taken to the streets. Put themselves at risk. Young and old, mothers, fathers, grandmothers, grandfathers, kids. We're not revolutionaries. There is no window breaking or rioting on our part. We're just parents, responsible people, who are against this war and decided to do something to make it stop. Amen."

"Amen….And how are you, old buddy? What about the bad dreams?"

"I still get 'em. I'll never get that day out of my system. It comes back. Same old stuff. Why them, not me. Why my little brother Johnny, who I always looked after, and not me? I've had a life and he hasn't. I see Jimbo getting shot up as he tried to scale the conning tower. It keeps coming back. My brain still carries the smell of burning flesh. It's still there."

"Bob. Listen to me. Go to the VA. You need to do it. It's been over thirty years. You don't have to put up with this anymore. I got help and got it out of my system. So can you."

"You and Katie don't let up. Davey, I simply cannot talk about that day. I can't. I won't. Please. Don't bug me about it anymore. Please!"

"Ok. Alright. Let's move on. You coming this way this summer? I've got a new boat, just right for tuna."

"I'll be there if you want me. How about late July?"

"You're on. Late July is fine."

A month later, on the boat off Savannah..

"You know about the survivor association, Bob. Close to one hundred members, apparently. You may want to get in touch with it." Bob and Davey were having a beer on the way back from a day on the water, Davey under a full brimmed hat to protect his face, Bob wearing his favorite beat-up red Kansas City Chiefs baseball cap. "It may help you. Probably could. See some of the old guys. I'm sure many of them have had the same problems as us. Would be good for you to see, hear, what they have done with it. May be cathartic. Something different than talking to a shrink."

"No, Davey. I won't. Back off of this stuff. I don't want to hear about it."

"Ok."

The phone rang. Bob was preparing steaks on the grill, while Davey was fixing drinks. "Bob, call for you. It's Katie." Bob took the phone. "My dear, what's up? Having a great time here, by the way."

"Something's wrong with John. Bad fever. Convulsions. I'm calling from the hospital. I don't like it. You'd better come home."

"Convulsions. Fever. My God. He was OK two days ago before I left."

"This morning. He called for me, said he was not well. I went to his room, stayed with him. I had to do an errand, but I thought he would be OK. Put him on the back porch, to get some air. When I came back around three, I took his temperature. 104. He was perspiring all over. He was retching, convulsing. I called an ambulance. Got here a half hour ago, Bob. Come home. I don't like this."

"OK. I will fly this evening. Which hospital is it?"

"St. Francis. I'm staying here until I know more."

Bob put down the phone. "Something wrong with my son. Gotta get back, Davey. Katie very worried. And she's a nurse. Can you take me to the airport? I need to get home tonight."

Later that evening…

"He's got viral pneumonia, Bob. It's bad. He may have spinal meningitis as well, according to the doctor. He's in and out of consciousness. He could die."

"He could die? What are you talking about? People 28 years old are not supposed to die from pneumonia."

"Bob, I'm a nurse. I know. Meningitis with pneumonia could kill him. The doctor said it could happen, although they are doing everything they can. They are pouring in antibiotics. He's weak, has been since he came back. I can't bear losing him." His wife was in tears as he held her hand in the hall outside his son's room.

"We won't lose him, Katie."

"You let him go. You let him go to Vietnam. He could have waited, to see if he was drafted. You said no, best to enlist before that. I knew it would happen."

"I need to see him. I'm going in."

"He's sedated. I'm going downstairs to get something to eat."

Bob walked into the room. His son was hooked up to a machine and had a drip into his arm. He took John's hand. A second later, John opened his eyes and looked over at his father, startling him. "You escaped, Dad. You got through it all. Will I?"

Bob was taken aback. Katie had told him he was sedated, unresponsive. John was awake and looking directly at him. "You will, John. You will make it through this. You have to fight. Fight back. You can do it."

"Come on, Dad. My life is a shambles. It's unbearable. I am in pain all the time. I have not complained much about it to you and Mom, but I've told the doctor about it. It's not just pneumonia, Dad. Something else is happening to me. I lose feeling in my hands. Off and on. I get numbness in my neck.....Crazy stuff. But it's not just the body, Dad. It's the soul. I'm in a wheelchair. I always will be. I'm deteriorating."

"Fucking war. I can never escape this. I will be like this forever. I might as well be dead...." He looked off towards the window. "It's dark outside. It's dark all the time now. How did you escape the pain, Dad? War. You made it through it. You escaped it."

"I didn't escape it, John. There are things you don't know."

"Things I don't know.......what are you talking about?"

"You should know. It's about time. You only know part of my involvement in the war." Bob looked at his son and realized at that moment that what he was about to say would be a liberation. He hesitated a moment. *It's about time. This one needs to know. But only him.* "I will tell you more. But you have to promise me that it stays with you. I don't want David or anybody else to know what I am going to tell you. Can you promise me that?"

"Why me and not David?"

"I just don't want to have to talk about it. It's a long time ago. Let's just leave it at that. Maybe someday I will tell him. Promise?"

"OK. Promise."

"Here it is. But I never want to talk about it again....I was not always an officer, landing troops on beaches, John. At the beginning of the war, I was an ordinary seaman on a ship that was based at Pearl Harbor. It was the Arizona. John, your uncle you never knew, for who you were named, was also there, on another ship."

"The Arizona? It blew up, Dad. You were on the Arizona?"

"Yes, I was. I survived the attack...obviously. Most didn't. Including Johnny on his destroyer. The memory of it and why I got through it and so many guys didn't has tormented me

116

all my life. I haven't escaped, John. The pain is still there. It doesn't go away."

"Why didn't you tell us? It would have been good for me to know. For David to know, although I will keep the promise. There has always been something missing with you, Dad. Something we could never put our finger on. At times you were so, so distant. We would be at a ballgame; in a boat on a lake and you would be off in thought. As if you weren't there. We saw it so many times. We would ask Mom. She would never level with us. Told us not to question you. Just said you had a side to you that was just you and we should accept it. We knew there was something, something that really ate at you."

"Yes, I had secrets. Stuff I didn't ever want to talk about."

"All about the war. About the part you never told us about."

"Yes, all about the war. I couldn't tell you, John. I have tried to forget everything about it. For over thirty years. Put it out of my mind, out of my being. Men burning alive. Screams. Bodies in the water. Parts of bodies. It has never left me."

"Mom. Where was she in all of this?"

"I met your wonderful mother, the love of my life, the day before the attack. She knows it all, of course. About my problem with the memory of it. She was in Honolulu the day of the attack. A Navy nurse. Saw a lot of broken guys. Worked to patch them up as best she and the others could. We had a pact, something I insisted upon. I made her promise before we were married to never mention anything about the Arizona and my being on it to anyone. Ever. She has kept the promise. It has not been easy on her."

"You knew her then. I thought you met after the war."

"It was the day before. On the beach. A lovely Saturday afternoon. I was smitten with your mother right away. We ended up going to a band concert that evening and had a wonderful time. I was bowled over in love with her. The same as today. Always. But....December 6, 1941. Moonlight Serenade on the beach in Hawaii. A couple of kids in paradise. We had no idea of what was coming. Nobody did."

"We lost touch after the attack. I was in hospital for awhile with burns and a bad knock on my head. But she thought I was dead. The Arizona. Everybody knew about that. She met someone else in the days after the attack and ended up marrying him. You don't know that. But the guy was killed in action a year or so after they were married. She continued to work as a nurse in Hawaii. I found her after the war. In the meantime, I had come back to Kansas after Pearl but wanted to get back in it. Revenge. Kill as many Japs as I could. But as an officer. Got accepted to officer candidate school and ended up in charge of the LCT in the Pacific, landing troops on beaches. That's what you and David know. Now you know the rest."

John looked at his father. "Fate. Destiny. It's all about fate, Dad. You were fated to survive. I wasn't."

"You're not dead, John. You are a survivor. You can still live a good life."

"No, Dad. I went out that morning. I didn't have to. Somebody else was supposed to check the runway. If I had gone

118

into the office instead, I would not have been on the tarmac. Just like you that day. Fate. Why? Why, Dad?"

"I don't know, son. I don't know."

At that moment, Katie walked into the room. "Hey, you're awake." She saw it. Felt it. Something was happening. Bob turned, then looked away. John avoided her gaze. He was looking at the foot of the bed. Staring at it. "I.....I. Looks like I came in on something. John, are you OK? You're awake."

"I'm OK, Mom. OK."

Bob spoke up. "Where is the doctor? Can I see him?" He did not know what else to say. The moment had been intense.

"He's somewhere. I'll get him." Katie hurriedly left the room. She knew she had intruded. Her men were talking. It had stopped. She did not want it to stop. She left the room.

"You're not going to die, John," said Bob as the door closed. "You have everything to give in life. You have everything to give. There is still a full life for you out there. Fight for it."

Chapter 16

Katie had great difficulty in dealing with her son's death and sought professional help to deal with it. She had lost a husband to war and now a son. At many times she was afraid she was losing her second husband as well, if not in body, then in spirit, even as she was proud of him for mobilizing people against the war.

"Bob, I am so proud of you for doing what you are doing. David is so proud of you. But, you need to deal with your problem. You bolted up in bed again last night. You were yelling. But you were not awake. Did you know what you were doing?"

"I know. It was the dream again."

"It's just like so many other times. You have to deal with this, Bob. We have always had problems disguising this over the years. But David knows there is something wrong. He always has known there is something that drives you to be so distant. He has heard your voice at night. I have always deflected questions about it. You know that. I promised you I would keep the stuff about Pearl and that day away from everyone, and I have. But it has been difficult and I can't do it anymore. You have kept all of this bottled up inside you and away from the boys. I take the brunt of it. Can't talk about it, you say. It's hell. I can't take it. I have to look after me. I've tried with you. You have to get over it. Maybe John's passing will move you to it. If you don't start dealing with it, I will leave you. I mean it. In the meantime, I am seeing a therapist. To deal with the loss of my son."

The following day, Bob was at the Veterans' Administration hospital in Topeka and asking for help. "The horror and the guilt has consumed me for too long. I have to end it," he told the psychologist. "I need to save me, my marriage, the rest of my family, my life. It's been thirty years. So damn long. I'm here and I need help."

Over the next year, Bob went through extensive therapy, with sessions every two weeks. He managed to do it around his speaking activities. At the end of the year, he believed he had come to terms with his condition. The nightmares had stopped. The relationship with Katie had improved.

In the meantime, Bob continued the organization of resistance to the war. Parents-Against-the-War was a movement and Bob was the leading spokesman for it. He continued to appear on television; in interviews with leading commentators, both local and national. He was interviewed on The David Brinkley show and with Dan Rather on CBS. There was mention of him being a veteran, but no mention of Pearl Harbor or the Arizona.

He had been a warrior, and now he was against it all. "I'm proud of you, Dad," said David one day in a call home. "Washington is changing. We can sense it. Nixon is giving signs he wants to stop it."

Chapter 17

March 1973

The telephone rang. Bob looked at his watch. It was 10:45 pm. Who could be calling at this hour? He picked it up. "Is this Robert Kane?" asked the heavy voice. "Yes, it is. Who is calling?"

"Missouri State Police, Mr. Kane. Your wife has been involved in a road accident, sir. She has been taken to hospital in Columbia."

"A road accident. Where? When did it happen?"

"Approximately an hour ago, sir. On highway 54 not far from Interstate 70."

"Is it serious?"

"Yes it is, I'm sorry to say."

"Is she alive?"

"I can't confirm her condition, sir. All I can tell you is that she was taken to University Hospital in Columbia with multiple injuries. I suggest you call the hospital. I have the number here."

"What happened, officer? What can you tell me?"

"Her car entered into a head-on collision with a vehicle coming the other way. Two lane highway not far from the Interstate. I can't tell you all the circumstances at this time. I can tell you, however, that it was raining at the time. We are not sure what happened."

Katie had gone to see her mother who had moved back to Hannibal a few years before. Bob dialled the hospital.

"Sir, I suggest you come here."

"You can't tell me how she is?

"Sir, you have to come here."

"Is she alive?"

"Hold on. I will put you through to the emergency MD, sir."

"Mr. Kane, your wife didn't make it, I'm sorry to say. Massive head injuries. Severe trauma. We couldn't save her. I'm sorry."

"I'm coming to Columbia, doctor. I will be there in 90 minutes."

"I will be on duty. Please ask for me. I'm sorry, sir."

Chapter 18

A week later, Bob was on the phone with his old friend. "Davey, Katie was not the same after John's death. The twenty months or so since his passing were not easy for her. She took it hard. She lost her first husband to war and then a son. And she was always afraid David would somehow get drafted and fulfill his promise to go to Canada and would not be around. That worry ended when Congress said things in Vietnam had to end along with the draft, but then John got sick with pneumonia and meningitis and she couldn't save him."

"I'm really sorry for you, buddy. You two started at Pearl. I still remember that evening on the dance floor when I saw you together. You were some happy guy. I'm so sorry for you and for your son. How's he doing?"

"Not easy for him. You know, Davey, her saving grace in the passing of John, was David. He was great for her, stayed close, a rock. He decided to pursue graduate school close by, at Kansas in Lawrence, to be around. But, she never got over losing John. She spent more time with her mother after that. I still can't figure out why she got into her car that rainy night to come home. Her mother told me she just got up and said she was leaving. Went and got her things, threw them in the car and took off. Her mother tried to get her to wait until the morning, but Katie insisted on doing it then. Strange. Was it fate for her to take the road that night? I don't know. It's almost as if she wished it to happen."

"What about you in all of this?"

"I feel responsible. For years I was self-absorbed. Caught up in my business and then I wouldn't listen to her about getting help for my war stuff and all of that. It helped when I finally got into treatment, but it was so long in coming. She put so much into the boys. It was devastating when the oldest died. I tried to fill the void, but she was such a devoted mother. I couldn't make up for it and I was late in going for help. Very late. I'm having trouble dealing with it all."

"What are you going to do now?"

"I don't know, Davey. She was the love of my life. I could have done such a better job in showing it over the years. But God, did I love her. From the first time I saw her, right to the last. You know, old buddy, the war was so destructive for us. It stayed with me. I could never release myself from it. I have improved on that, but it cost me with Katie. There were so many times I was not around. I mean in my mind not around. She put up with it. I am so sorry about that. I'm fifty-three. I still have a ways to go, but I really don't know what I am going to do. There is just such emptiness."

Bob and David Kane were travelling back from Hannibal after a visit with Katie's mother. It had been a month since the accident. The gracious lady who Bob had always liked had not been well, devastated like everyone with Katie's death. She felt responsible, not succeeding in keeping her daughter from taking the road that night. She had always liked Bob and was grateful for the visit. Bob knew that contact would be less frequent now and he regretted that, vowing to do whatever he could to stay close.

"Just the two of us now, son. We'll have to make the best of it. You have to continue with what you are doing and not worry about me."

"I do worry about you, Dad. You haven't been the same since Mom died. Even more than I thought."

"Well, she was everything to me. I wish I had shown it more. Now about you going forward. We should talk about that. We haven't in a while."

"I'm OK, Dad. But about you. And not just about Mom and your time with that since then. You had troubles over the years. All those times when we were little and you were off somewhere in thought or whatever. You were there, but you often weren't. We sensed it, we knew it, but Mom told us not to worry. You were busy, had a business to run. You said the same thing the times we asked you what was bothering you. It was more than that, more than business, wasn't it, Dad?"

"It was that, but you know, David, I saw things in the war that mark you forever."

"Landing troops and all that? Weren't you in Japan after the war?"

"I was there, but not for very long. Whatever I saw in the war I have tried to forget. David, I really don't want to talk about

126

it. Please respect that. It has taken a long time to get those things out of my mind."

"You had therapy, didn't you Dad? I followed you once. To the VA in Topeka."

"So you followed me. Yes, I did go. Many times over a year. It helped and I'm glad I did it, but it's over now. I don't want to talk about it. It's done. Millions of men were scarred by war. I was no different. Please respect that, David. It has not been easy."

"OK. At least I know where it came from." *No, you don't, son.* "I will respect that, Dad."

"Now, we haven't really talked about your grad school and career stuff. What do you want to do? Money should not be an issue. I have turned over the proceeds from your mother's life insurance policy to you. I don't need the money. You will need some, and Mom would have wanted it that way, anyway. You should invest whatever you don't need for the rest of your studies. Be smart about it. Invest it, get a head start on financial security."

"I will. Being an insurance man's son should give me some insights, some rules to follow."

"So, what do you want to do? We haven't talked about this for awhile. Master's degree in History. Where do you want to go with that?"

"I want to teach, Dad. We've talked about that. Teach history. I'm fascinated by it, always have been. You suggested I go for a degree in economics when I started out after high school, but it was not for me. Business was not for me, either. So, history became my major, my post-graduate thing as well and I want to continue in it. Get a PhD. Work in academia."

"That sounds good. It's you. History, political science. I think you can make something of it. Would be a good life."

"Washington U. in St. Louis has a great doctoral program in European history. And, I've heard about a great program in medieval European history at the University of Milan. There are options out there. I want to check them out. I will see where it takes me."

"Good, David. I'm behind you. Go for it. In the meantime, we've got tickets to the Royals-Indians game tomorrow night. Let's have a beer or two and some fun before you go back."

"Right on, Dad. Sounds good."

Chapter 19

Three years later, San Francisco

"Hello, Bob Kane, you probably don't remember me, but I was in the Parents-Against-the-War chapter when you came here to give a talk a few years ago. We had a meeting and had a chat afterwards. Just want to say hello. I am so glad you got all that going and of course we did it." Bob was alone having dinner in the restaurant of the hotel. He had concluded another deal near Napa earlier that day, the fifth one in the area over the last two years. He vaguely remembered the striking woman who had come over to his table from where she was sitting with two other women.

"Yes, I think I do remember. What is your name?"

"Ruth. Ruth Ellis. Just here with some girl friends. Girls night out. I just thought I would come by and say hello."

"Very good, Ruth. Glad to see you. A lot has happened since our marches and rantings and all that."

"Bob, you know I would be interested in talking about it sometime, if we could, as a matter of fact. There is a lot that I did not know, about what was going on. Behind the scenes. I'm sure there was a lot and you were most likely in the middle of it. I've always been curious about it."

'Well, I'm here. I have nothing going on this evening. Be glad to talk about it. You are welcome to join me here. Supper won't take long. You're welcome. We can talk right here."

"I think I'll do that. I'll tell the girls they can go on without me. We were done anyway. Be back."

Ruth came back to the table a few minutes later and they would talk for an hour, but not all about Parents-Against-the-War.

"So much for all those goings-on," said Bob. "But I had to do it. I was already a speaker. I just needed to change the subject, and I'm glad I did. What happened to your son, Ruth? You had one of that age for you to be involved, I would think. Did you have one that went over there? Did he make it?"

"Yes, he did. In the Air Force. He made it back OK. He was furious with me at the start, when I got involved with PATW. But not at the end. He had seen it all. It was enough."

"What about you? Your husband, his father? He's not here, although it's girl's night out. How did he feel about it?"

'My husband died eight years ago. Cancer. Long before the boys were vulnerable to it all. It's just been me and my boys since then."

"I'm sorry to hear that, Ruth....your husband. About your boys. You have more than one."

"Yes, I have another one. He's very different from the oldest one who now teaches and coaches high school football, across the bay in Berkeley where I live. James, the second son, is a convert to Buddhism. He lives in Taipei. He went over there one summer when he was in college and decided to go back. He writes about Eastern religions now and makes documentaries with his wife who is Chinese. Taiwan Chinese. The boys have taken very different paths. They are close, just the same. What about your family, Bob?"

"I have just one son now. The oldest one was in Vietnam, got shot in the wrong place and died of complications from it. My wife died a few years ago in a car accident. David, the son who is left, is working towards a doctorate in history at a university in Italy. And I am here looking into some real estate deals. What do you do, Ruth? Do you work?"

"I'm a nurse and I still work. Can't afford to quit."

"My wife was a nurse as well."

"Looks like we have a few things in common."

"Looks like we do. Shall we get together again, Ruth? I have enjoyed our talk."

"Why not, Bob. Yes, I would like that. I'm glad I saw you tonight." She had a twinkle in her eye. She had had it ever since she had sat down at the table.

"I've got an idea. On Saturday, I need to go down to Monterey to check out a property. Why don't you come with me? We could have lunch down there and I would get you back by sundown. How about it?"

"I would love to do that. Where do I meet you? Here? Where do you live? I gather you don't live here at the hotel."

"No, I rent an apartment not far from here and I come to the hotel for dinner from time to time. I still have our house in Kansas City but come here on a regular basis. Why don't we meet here at the hotel? 9 o'clock on Saturday in the lobby. OK?"

"OK."

Bob Kane and Ruth Ellis were having lunch. Bob had spotted the restaurant overlooking the ocean just outside the town on a previous trip. The glass enclosed restaurant had an amazing view of the bay and the rugged coast. "There are some beautiful places around here, Ruth, up in the hills and along the coast. And I love driving up and down Highway 1. The beaches are stupendous. I'm thinking of moving here."

"You don't have anything left in Kansas City? What about your son?"

"He's in Italy now. Probably will end up in Europe or at a university back east. He met an Italian girl and married her last year. I'm pretty sure he won't be coming back to Kansas. I'm going to be a grandfather soon, by the way. My wife and oldest son are buried in Kansas City and that may be the one last thing that keeps me from moving completely out here. I have a dear aunt back there who was a second mother to me in my teens, but I don't know how long she will still be around. She's 82. I don't want to get too far away from her, but I'll probably be here before long. You saw that place on the other side of town, up the hill. Pretty nice, huh?"

"Yes, pretty nice. A bit big for you, maybe?"

"Maybe, but I may make a bid for it. Anyway, tell me about your boys."

"One's pretty conventional, the other less so, you might say. Carter was always into sports and James into more intellectual pursuits. They have followed that pattern. Both married. I am a grandmother to two. James and his wife don't have children yet."

"And your husband?"

"He worked in technology. He became an engineer after the war and worked for a long time for a semiconductor company. Things were good, life was good, but he was diagnosed with cancer of the lymph nodes during a routine checkup. He was gone within two years. Doctors said it probably came from the war. He was part of the occupation in Japan."

"So was I."

"You were? With the army?"

"No, the Navy. I got out of there as soon as I could. Your husband was probably exposed to toxic stuff. I saw a lot of that."

"Yes, he was. He was stationed not far from Nagasaki. But he could never prove the link with his cancer and I gave up trying to do it after his death. It was awful."

Later that afternoon, back in San Francisco. "Well, here we are. It's been nice, Ruth."

"Yes, it has." Ruth turned to Bob before opening the car door. "Do we see each other again, Bob?"

"Yes, I would like that."

"Well then, how about a movie tomorrow night, before you go back? The theatre down the street. Couple of good movies playing. There's the one about Nixon and Watergate with Robert Redford."

"I know a bit about that man. He wouldn't meet with us. Good. Great idea. Let's do that. We meet here in the lobby once again. Come early. We'll have dinner first."

"OK. See you at 6 tomorrow."

The next evening, after the movie with Ruth taking Bob's hand as they crossed the street to the hotel….

"Do we have a nightcap, Bob?"

"Yes, I think we could," as he looked over at Ruth, knowing full well what she meant.

"Maybe we should have it in the room. What do you think?" Ruth turned to Bob before they went through the door to the lobby. "I don't want to go home tonight."

"You don't have to. Let's go."

Bob returned two weeks later. He and Ruth spent the weekend in Monterey. They had spoken on the telephone six times in the interim.

Some time later, after another visit, Bob was on the phone with his son. "David, I believe I have found a companion. I hope it won't upset you."

"It's about time, Dad. Mom would not be upset. It's been three years. A long time to be alone. No one deserves to be alone forever. You sound happy."

"I am, but I don't want to harm the legacy of your mother. She was everything to me. No one will ever replace her. I trust you know that."

"I do, Dad. Don't worry. I do. Tell me about the lady."

"Well, she's a fine person and I think you'll like her......

Bob Kane and Ruth Ellis were married four months later in San Francisco. David was his dad's best man. With him was Luciana, the beautiful Italian girl from Siena he had married the year before, along with Bob's three month old grandson, named after him but with everyone calling him Roberto or Robbie. The names would stick.

Chapter 20

Twenty three years later, January 1999…

"Dad, Roberto is getting married. A lovely girl he met a few months ago in Osaka. We haven't met her yet, but she seems to be quite a wonderful, intelligent young lady."

Bob hesitated for a moment. "Is she Japanese?"

"Yes, she is. Apparently from Kyoto. Roberto met her at the university."

Bob did not say anything. A long moment passed.

"Dad, are you all right? You still there?"

"Yeah, I'm here. I'm OK."

"You don't sound happy about it. Your one grandson getting married. Big moment, Dad."

Bob righted himself. "No, David, I'm happy for Robbie. Very happy for him. When is the wedding?"

"Second Saturday in May. In Kyoto. Luciana, the girls and I will of course be there. You and Ruth will certainly be going as well. You can't miss that."

"I don't know, David. For God's sake, I'm 79 now. Quite a trip. I'll have to talk to Ruth."

David sensed his father's reticence. "Is this about the war, Dad? About Japan and your feelings about Japan? The stuff you have always avoided talking about. Huh, Dad? If it is, you'd better get over it. Because you are going to have some of Japan in your family, our family."

"David, I will talk to Ruth."

"Why don't you want to go to Japan, Bob? It's your grandson's wedding." Bob did not answer. He and Ruth were in the kitchen. She had heard Bob's end of the conversation and had seen his reaction.

"Still about the war, is it? It's been over fifty years, Bob. Time to get over it. You love that boy."

"I'm not going. It's too far, takes too long, I'm too old. And Ruth, it's not about the war."

"Bob Kane, you are as healthy as a horse. You can go to Paris and Rome on a whim, but you can't go to your own grandson's wedding in Kyoto. Come on, this is about the war and it's about time you let it go. You will regret it. And what are you going to tell Robbie?"

"Ruth, I'm not going. I was involved in the occupation in Japan and I don't want to go back there. Final. I won't. It'll be about health."

"What are you going to do, fake a stroke or something? This doesn't make any sense, Bob."

"You can go, Ruth. Represent us. Please don't ask me to do it. I will think of something to tell Robbie and David."

Three days later..

"Grandpa. I hear you're not coming to my wedding. What is this? Ruth says something about your health."

"Robbie, I'm happy for you, but I'm getting old. Worried about something happening. Have to be careful now. Strains of a long trip."

"Your health? Come on, Grandpa. When I saw you last summer, we walked eighteen holes, two days in a row at those courses at Pebble Beach. You insisted on it. Got an exemption from the requirement to use a cart. What has changed since then? Dad saw you at Christmas and said you looked great. Said you guys had a game of squash. Come on! You gotta be here. It's a direct flight now to Osaka. I'll pick you up. You will have a great place at the hotel. I guarantee it. You will love Kumi. I would be very disappointed if you weren't here. You have to be here."

Bob was silent for a moment.

"OK, Robbie. I will be there. Ruth and I will be there. I will be careful. So when is it exactly and when should we be there?"

On the highway from Osaka, three months later..

Ruth and Bob were with Roberto who had picked them up. "Well, Robbie, tell us about the girl you are marrying," asked Ruth. Bob had been silent since they had been in the car.

"She's a graduate student at Osaka University. In another program, but was taking an English language economics course that I was taking as well. She sat next to me. I was attracted to her right away, but she was very shy at the start. It took a while."

"It usually does with smart women" said Ruth. "And…?"

"I would try to talk to her but she would not respond other than say hello. One day I asked her to have tea with me after class and she said yes. I don't know what it is about the girls here with Western guys, but they seem to keep their distance. Later, she told me about that. They apparently think us a bit brutish. Anyway, it turned out she spoke excellent English, had a funky sense of humour and we hit it off. She was also beautiful. I fell for her like a ton of bricks, Grandpa. I think you will like her a lot."

"What's her family like? You've probably met them," asked Bob, breaking his silence.

"Her father is a business executive. Works for a big company here. Very much a business family on her father's side. Her mother's side is more traditional and is from Kyoto. Land holdings and that. There is no want for money in the two families, as far as I can tell. They are paying for everything. Kumi has two sisters, both younger than her. I get along great with her father, who I think is glad to have another male around, and is happy I believe that his daughter is marrying somebody who will be in the business world. He has said he is anxious to meet you and Dad, by the way. He and Kumi's mother are visiting with Mom and Dad at the hotel as we speak. I guess you and Ruth are next to be inspected. Things are that way here."

The car was passing the sign for Kobe in Japanese and English. Bob didn't miss it.

Bob fell silent once again as they continued along the highway. "What are you two going to do? Where are you going to live?' asked Ruth, breaking the silence.

"Kumi wants to teach. She will have a Master's degree next year. I may work here but I will probably find my way back to the U.S. before long. Having an international business degree from Japan will be valuable for U.S. firms targeting Asia. Kumi realizes that and does not object to us living in the United States. She will not have a problem finding a job, I am sure."

Bob did not say anything. He had few words to say the rest of the one hour ride to Kyoto. Later that evening, after dinner in the hotel restaurant, Bob took his grandson aside. "Your fiancée is wonderful, my boy. She's a jewel. You are a lucky young man."

"Now, grandson who has grown up so fast, what will be the religion of the ceremony? I understand it will be at a reception hall. No shrine? No church? It's Japan. I thought it would be at a shrine."

"Kumi and her parents thought it would be better for all if the ceremony were not so religious. In any case, more and more weddings here happen in the Western tradition. For one, you do not need a ceremony in Japan for a marriage to be officialised. People getting married just need to sign a marriage consent and have it registered. Less and less marriages are celebrated in shrines."

"Anyway, Kumi's family wanted us to be comfortable and relaxed, and they found a really nice place for it. A friend of the family will act as minister. Afterwards we will have a banquet in an adjoining area of the hall. Pretty much like home or in Europe."

The next day, after the ceremony and before everyone had taken their places at the banquet table, Bob and his grandson found themselves in the men's room. "Robbie, there was an elderly gentleman dressed in what looked like traditional robes sitting just behind Kumi's parents. Very elegant dress. Who was he? Do you know? I noticed he's sitting not far from me at the table."

"That's Kumi's grandfather. Father of her mother. He is a Shinto priest. You will meet him. He speaks excellent English."

Chapter 21

Although he liked the young man his granddaughter was marrying, Keiji Hakagawa was not happy about her marriage to an American. He would have preferred she marry Japanese. But he did nothing to discourage it. He had loved America as a young man before the war and had been disturbed by what he had done at Pearl Harbor. He knew nothing about the war service of the other grandfather, Robert Kane. He suspected he had one. He was of that age, but his granddaughter knew nothing of it. With that, he suspected Kane's grandson may know nothing of it either. He had been told an uncle of his granddaughter's husband had been crippled in the war in Vietnam and had died young. A sensitive subject in the Kane family, apparently causing the young man's father and grandfather to have been very publicly vocal in their opposition to that war. The older man had even led a nationwide parents movement in opposition to it. On his side, his grandchildren including Kumi knew nothing about his own wartime service. The subject was taboo in the family. Apart from his two sisters and his wife, nobody else knew anything about it. His children were never told of his Pearl Harbor or Midway battles or anything involved with his military service. After his father died in 1945, everything about his time in the military had been expunged. Buried. He had been a holy man since 1948 and only wanted to be known for that. His wife and sisters never betrayed it.

The two elderly gentlemen were seated across from each other at an angle. Early in the dinner, their eyes met. The Japanese man bowed his head slightly in Bob's direction. Bob returned the gesture. After the dinner was over with, Bob approached the man and they shook hands. The Japanese man spoke first. "Welcome to Japan, Mr. Kane. You have a fine grandson. We are proud to have him in our family." Despite the warmth of the man's words and his solemn declaration, Bob was uncomfortable. "I thank you, sir. I am glad you feel that way."

Bob and Ruth returned to California two days later. The two elderly grandfathers did not manage to speak again after their brief conversation.

On the plane before they took off from Osaka, Ruth turned to Bob as they were fastening their seat belts and asked him "Was it all that bad, Bob?"

"No, it wasn't. I actually had a good time. I like her and she has a nice family. Robbie is happy and so is David. I'm good."

"I think this did you good."

"I think you're right."

Two months after their return, Ruth went for a routine bi-annual checkup. A colonoscopy suggested by her doctor showed she had colon cancer. She had had no symptoms and to that point in her life at age 76, had never had any serious medical problems. Surgery removed the tumor, but doctors detected the spread of the cancer elsewhere. Radiation therapy, then chemotherapy ensued. The treatments prolonged her life, but within eighteen months, Ruth was dead.

Ruth had told Bob before she died that she wanted to be buried next to her parents in Columbus, Ohio.

Over the years they had been married, Bob had become close to Ruth's boys. Carter, the oldest, lived in the Bay area and he and Bob shared a passion for sports. They played golf together regularly and went to baseball and football games, accompanied by Carter's kids and David and Robbie whenever they were around. James, the younger of the boys, had moved to Hong Kong from Taiwan a few years before but came to California at least once a year to see his mother. He would also meet with publishers and media organizations regarding documentaries and other materiel related to his work on Eastern religions. The boys in turn liked Bob and had considered him to be their substitute father.

Waiting for his plane to take him from Columbus to Savannah to visit again with his buddy Davey Poole after Ruth's burial, the thought once again came to him as it had a few times in the days before. Where will I put my own remains? Kansas City, with Katie and John? Topeka? Silver Lake with mom and dad? California, where he had lived the past twenty plus years? Columbus, with Ruth? Not really appropriate. Most likely next to Katie and John in Kansas City.

"So you went to Japan? You managed to get over it." Bob and his old friend were having a beer on Davey's covered porch in Old Savannah.

"Yes, I did," replied Bob. "I really didn't want to do it, but Robbie put it on me. I went. I must say the images came

144

back. The car ride on the way to Kyoto went past the runoff to Kobe, where I was stationed after the surrender. The horror of it all came back. One image after another. Difficult ride. I got over it. Still, it was tough."

"The family he married into over there is alright. I was OK through it, in the end. It was good I did it."

"Now you've buried Ruth. Second one. Where are you gonna put your bones? What are we now, 82?" said Davey.

"You may be, but I'm only 80. I'm not going to the maker soon, unless I get hit by a car or something. Doctor says I'm a specimen."

"We all are. All of us who survived. Anyway, I'm going to be buried with the boys. Down in the hull with them. My ashes. Decided to do it. No wife, no kids. Just me and nobody to lament they won't be able to be with me."

"What? What are you talking about?"

"You don't know. I gather you really don't open those letters from the survivors' association. Over fifteen guys who survived that day with us have had their ashes lowered into the ship, to be with the guys. I'm going to have the same done with mine. I actually feel pretty good about it."

"You're serious. You are going to go back there for eternity."

"Yep. That day marked my life. Those guys are all still down there, what's left of them. I lived, they didn't. They deserve to be honoured. My way of doing it along with, it looks like, a few others. It's only fitting. A supreme gesture of respect. That's how I see it."

"Well, I'm not going to do it. I can't bear the thought of going anywhere near the place."

On the way back to California, in the plane looking out over the heartland of America from thirty five thousand feet, with the multitude of farms and fields stretching as far as the eye could see, the thought came back to him. Honor his buddies, our buddies. Supreme gesture of respect. I couldn't do that.

Chapter 22

Bob saw there was a message on his telephone at the house. "Bob, listen, this is Jamie. I have to be in San Francisco next week. Coming to see you. I'll be there next Tuesday around supper time. We'll go to that favourite restaurant of yours on the wharf. It'll be on me, but please make the registration. Ciao." It had been three months since Ruth's passing and Bob was glad to hear from James. Great. Will be glad to see the boy, thought Bob as he put down the phone, even though James was hardly a boy, at 49 years of age.

The following Tuesday Bob and James took their seats on the balcony of the restaurant overlooking Monterey Bay. "James, I loved your mother. I hope you know that. I loved her even though my first wife was so much a part of me. Your mother knew that, and I knew she always loved your dad. We shared our grief. But we had a great twenty five years together."

"I know that, Bob. You were good to her. Let's have a beer. And do a toast to them all."

"Yes, sir. I agree. Here's to your mom, your dad, and to my own Katie."

"Let's move on. I've got a question for you. More than one, actually. Robbie's wife's grandfather, on her mother's side, is a Shinto priest. You know all about the Eastern religions. Shinto priests can marry, apparently. Not like our Catholic priests here. What's that religion all about? Who is their God? What is the premise of their faith? "By the way, I think you will be invited to the party Robbie is putting together for here in August. He and Kumi live in Palo Alto now, as you probably know."

"Yes, I know. I spoke to Robbie a couple weeks ago," responded James. "He seems to be doing well. He told me he works for one of those IT companies attached to Stanford."

"I'm glad for him. He will go a long way. Anyway, he's just decided to have a big family party and make sure everybody on both sides comes to it, including the people from Japan, you guys and Luciana's folks from Italy. He wants to have it here in Monterey. Many people will be able to stay at the house. Lots of room."

"Ok. Sounds great. We may be able to make it. We will certainly try. A lot will depend on the meeting I have tomorrow. If it works with them, I will have to come back in a few months. Combine the two, hopefully. Let's order. I'm hungry."

After ordering their food, James got into the discussion about the Shinto religion. "Bob, your questions about the Shinto religion...It is a different sort of one. Very Japanese. Only Japanese, really. It focuses on ritual practices to be carried out solemnly to establish a connection between present-day Japan and its ancient past. It is what I would call an optimistic faith, with humans believed to be fundamentally good, and evil caused by evil spirits. Consequently, the purpose of most Shinto rituals is to keep away the bad spirits by purification, prayers and offerings to the kami. Kami are the spirits or phenomena that are worshiped in the religion of **Shinto**. They can be elements of the landscape, forces of nature, as well as beings and the qualities that these beings express, and include the spirits of venerated dead persons. Kami can be a dead person, such as a venerated Emperor. Kami are not visible to the human realm. Instead they inhabit sacred places, natural phenomena or people during rituals that ask for their blessing."

"Go on."

"Alright. The religion dates back to the fourth century B.C., but it has no founder, no overarching doctrine, nor religious texts. There is no real God as we know it in the Shinto religion. The deity for the Japanese is actually the Emperor. It is the religion of Japan, ethnically linked to the people. It's not practiced elsewhere in Asia. There are some Westerners who practice the Shinto faith, but they are few and far between. There are many Buddhists in Japan, but nowhere near the numbers of people who are of the Shinto faith. Mom told me when she came back from Japan with you that she read there were over 400 Shinto shrines in Kyoto. It is a very deep part of the Japanese heritage and collective psyche."

"What about the priests?"

"And, yes, Shinto priests can marry. Just about anyone can become a Shinto priest. Two years of training at a specialized university, although the examinations are rigorous and determine the grade of priest. Women can be priests. Goes back to the war and the years afterwards. They needed priests and so many men were gone, although there are fewer women in it now. The priesthood is very hierarchical, like just about everything else in Japan."

"Kumi's grandfather is the head priest of one of the largest shrines in Kyoto," said Bob. "Something about the man, though. He speaks perfect English. I was stunned."

Chapter 23

A few months later

The party had been going on since noon. It was Robbie and Kumi's get-together to celebrate the union of the two families. Everyone was in a festive mood, mingling, telling stories and getting to know people on the other side of the family. Language was not an impediment, as most people on Kumi's side spoke good English. Her parents, her grandparents on her mother's side, her two sisters, as well as a cousin who worked in San Francisco, were there. Bob, David and Luciana were there with their kids along with Carter and James with their spouses and Carter's children. Lunch was over. People were going down to the beach for the rest of the afternoon before going to Monterey for a light dinner around the pool at Bob's house. It was something that Bob had insisted upon and for which he had hired a caterer.

While others were in discussion after finishing the meal, Bob proposed to Kumi's grandfather, who he had not had a chance to speak with yet, that they get away and take a stroll on the beach at the bottom of the cliff.

"I accept. Very good idea," replied the man as he rose from the table.

"You have a limp. Age? Something else? Forgive me for proposing this walk," said Bob as they took their steps at the bottom of the stairway from the top of the cliff. "We could have stayed on the balcony back there. By the way, you can call me Bob."

"No problem with the leg. I have had it a long time. And you can call me Keiji."

"You speak excellent English. I would have thought a Japanese priest in your religion would not be so conversant in our American way of speaking. Forgive me if that offends you."

"It did not offend me at all. I studied here when I was young. In Oregon, at the University of Oregon. For two years. Before that, I learned English on my own. I very much enjoyed my stay and my time with Americans. And I am glad now to be able to be here in simple trousers, sandals and what you call a polo shirt."

"No robes."

"No, no robes. We only wear them in our holy places and for ceremonial occasions. Otherwise, a suit. We have to keep our appearances. I am glad I can do this here. It is a beautiful day, Bob, and I am very happy meeting you and all of your family."

Bob sensed a warmth about him. Serenity, wisdom, but also humility and sadness.

'How long have you been a priest, if I may ask?"

"Since I was a young man." Bob waited for a more precise answer but it didn't come.

Keiji in turn had recognized in Bob, from the first time he had observed him two years before, a man who had been hurt in life. Lost one wife, then a second. Robbie had told him a lot. The men were silent a moment as they walked further down the beach. Keiji then proceeded to surprise Bob.

"You are a sensitive man, Kane. You have been hurt in your life. It shows. Please don't be offended by my saying so."

"What are you getting at?" Bob asked in a friendly way...."We all have our secrets. I have mine although you must know I have lost two spouses and a son. You have your secrets as well, I am sure. We have a common family connection now. I am actually happy with that. I never thought I would be."

"You were not terribly happy with Roberto's marriage to my granddaughter. I sensed that the day of the wedding when we met. You were not as joyous as your son and your wife. I must say, however, that today has been very enjoyable and we are all appearing to have a nice time in each other's company."

"We are having a nice time. The marriage of our grandchildren is fine. I may have been concerned about that at one time but not now. You are fine people, but our generation in America have scars from our common past. You must know that, but you are a priest. You may know what our generation went through in the war, but you cannot know the scars of those who were actually in it." Bob was opening up about the war. For one of the few times to anyone in almost 50 years, apart from Davey and the people at the VA.

"Oh, yes I can, Bob. You don't know this, but I was in the war before becoming a priest. I have scars as well. They led me to become what I am."

Bob Kane had images running through his mind of the deck of the ship, the planes coming at him, the fire in the water, the landings on the islands, the images of young men dead on the beach, rolling gently with the waves as they lapped the shore before anybody managed to carry them away.

"What? You were in the war? What were you doing in the war, Keiji?" Bob felt a twinge of anger, a premonition of dread of where this exchange was going.

"I was in the Navy. An aviator. I saw men die. I saw many men die."

"Where did you see men die?"

The elderly Japanese man hesitated, looking at Bob. He sensed immediately he had gone too far, had disclosed too much, even if it was not a lot. "Bob, I do not want to go further in this. I am sorry I told you I was in the war. It was a mistake. It was a long time ago, another life."

"Keiji, I was in the war. You must know that by know. Actively trying to kill Japanese. I saw many men die. Friends, many friends. We have a common problem. You became a priest because of it. You just said that. I have been a wreck most of my life because of it. My oldest son was a victim of war. You are right. I am a sensitive man and I wear it with difficulty."

Keiji Hakagawa looked out at the ocean for a moment, sighed, then turned to the elderly American next to him. "What happened to you in the war, Bob? You tell me and then I will tell you what happened to me to turn me away from it all. We are too old to keep these things bottled up."

"I was on the Arizona. I was one of the survivors. You must know about the Arizona. Pearl Harbor, December 7 1941."

"Oh, my God."

"What? Keiji? Your reaction. Were you there?"

He hesitated a moment. But he couldn't hold back. "Yes, I was there." He looked at Bob Kane and tears began to roll down his aging cheeks.

"I was there."

"How were you there, Keiji? What did you do?"

"I cannot. It is too much. This is too much, Bob. Let us go back." Keiji turned to start to go back up the beach. "We must stop this discussion."

"No. What did you do? You were an aviator. You were dropping bombs, weren't you? Keiji, you were dropping bombs at Pearl Harbor. Tell me it's not true. Please tell me it's not true."

The Japanese man could not hold it back. "It is true."

"The Arizona?"

"Yes, the Arizona."

"How?"

"I was the commander of the squadron that attacked that ship. I never got over it. It was horrible. I was so sick afterwards, I could not function as a commander again."

"One of your planes dropped the bomb into the Arizona."

"Yes. And I never recovered from it."

The two men looked at each other. Hate flashed across Bob's face as he looked at the man who just admitted to being the assassin, the killer of his buddies, and of his youth in the seminal event of his life. But the look of hate slowly vanished from Kane's face, replaced by one of sorrow, of the pain of memory of what happened that day close to 60 years before and the obvious pain of the man in front of him - the old, frail Japanese man in front of him, crying as well and shaking, bending over to touch the sand to prevent himself from falling, who was not the enemy anymore. He was a compatriot in grief, in sorrow, in remorse and guilt. They took a long look at each other, glancing briefly out to sea beyond the beach to gather thoughts and hide the tears, then turned and approached each other, placing their hands on each other's shoulders, and wept. They looked at each other for a long moment. Bob spoke first. "How could this possibly happen, Keiji? This is beyond belief."

"Yes, beyond belief."

"I don't know what to say. I should hate you, but I don't. Like it or not, we are united through our offspring.....and now, unbelievably through the horror of those moments that morning. They have dominated my life. So difficult to live with."

"And they changed mine." replied Keiji. "We have nowhere to hide. No more secrets," he said as he looked out to sea. "Only the horrible memories. Now the incredible linkage of them to us. I am shaken." Keiji looked back at Bob with tears in his eyes.

156

"So am I, sir. That day. That morning."

"Yes, that day so long ago. I can still see the men in the water. It has never left me."

"You probably saw me. I was one of those men in the water, desperate to avoid the fire and burning oil." Bob paused for a moment, then continued. "You became a priest, Keiji, and I regret to say I became a killer. I went back after the treatment of my injuries and avenged my lost youth, my lost friends, my lost brother. I killed many of your men. I turned against war eventually, but it was not until the loss of my son that did it for me." Bob hesitated a moment, then continued. "No one in our families should know about this. It would be too much for them. David knows nothing of this, only of the effects of it on me over the years. He would be overwhelmed, learning of this connection of ours. So would Robbie. It would be difficult for them to deal with it."

"Yes, we must keep it to ourselves. It is too destructive. I don't want to speak of that day to anyone and I will not, except maybe to you, if you want."

"Keiji, I never want to talk about it again."

"Then we will not. Thank you."

But, as they walked back to the restaurant, both men knew that it was not over.

Chapter 24

Keiji, his wife, and the other members of his family had returned to Japan. David was with his father in the living room of the house in Monterey before returning with Luciana and their daughters to Boston the next day.

"Dad, you should open up with Kumi and her family. Get to know them, and through them, the good side of Japan. The bad side was a long time ago." Bob looked at his son, but did not say anything.

"I saw you walking with her grandfather on the beach. You touched each other. He bent down, touched the sand, then rose up and put his hands on your shoulders. Looks like you had some sort of exchange there."

"We did have a conversation, David. Between two old men. Just between two old men."

"You don't want to tell me."

"No, I don't. Between two old men. We'll leave it at that."

"OK. But I suggest you spend more time with Kumi. It would please Robbie, I am sure. He wants the two families to function well together."

"It has been a good start, so far. I'm all for it continuing. I like her family."

Bob was on the phone with his grandson the following evening. "Robbie, why don't you and Kumi come down here on Saturday. There is a great little Japanese restaurant in town now. You can stay here and go back on Sunday. Come on down, it's about time I got to know your wife a little more."

"Ok. Sounds good. We had nothing planned. Hold on. Kumi's not far." Robbie returned to the phone a moment later. "We're on, Grandpa. I'm glad you want to do this. Her family likes you and it looks like you hit it off with her grandfather. With her father as well."

"Yes, we had some good discussions. Two very different men, by the way."

"Well, very different family backgrounds, but Kumi can talk to you about that."

"Ok, so I will see you two Saturday. Come in the afternoon. We'll have a swim."

"Japan has not always been a pacifist nation, nor a peaceful one. As a matter of fact, we have much conflict and military activity in our past." Kumi was in the midst of talking of the history of her people.

"I know that. I fought against Japan a long time ago, which you probably should know by now."

"Yes, I know. You were part of the occupation after the war."

"There was more to it than that, but I don't want to talk about it. It's a long time ago, Kumi. But I would like to know about the other Japan, the one before this century."

"I suppose you would like to know what made us do what we did."

"Well, there is that. It would maybe help me exchange with your family. But it's more than that. I have avoided any mention of Japan, any contact with Japanese since 1945. We are now family. I want to know more."

"Do you mean about our history, our traditions?"

"Yes. Please. I would be grateful if you could."

"Ok. From the beginning. What every schoolchild is told. Japan was founded, according to myth, in the 7th century BC by our first emperor, Jimmu, a direct descendant of the Shinto sun goddess, Amaterasu. According to the legend, Jimmu started a line of emperors that remains to this day. Therefore, in that way, our Emperor is a deity, a direct descendant of a goddess in our religion."

"So, this is the foundation of what your grandfather preaches."

160

"Yes and no. Our priests do not preach. There are no pulpits in our shrines. They inform and educate. Shinto priests show by example the way to harmony with nature, with the spirits, with what are called kami, parts of our lives in the real world and in the abstract that form the basis of our identity as a people. Ceremonies and rituals carried out by our priests show a discipline of respect of nature, of personal discipline and rigor in daily life as well as respect of the Japanese identity and heritage."

"Jamie, Ruth's son, has told me about the Shinto religion. I wanted to know more about it in advance of the family get-together. What you two have told me appears to be the basis of a profoundly spiritual, non-violent approach to life. Where did the violent, warlike nature of Japan in the 20th century come from?"

"Japan has had periods of warrior culture. Not always but for long stretches just the same. It has had to defend itself from the beginning. Primarily from invasion from China. The Mongol hordes as well, who tried to conquer us. And to be successful in our defense, we Japanese had to be united. By necessity. We had to be stronger, more cunning. That usually meant unity by force, through powerful clans. You must know the Chinese, so much more numerous than us, and so close by, have been a continual threat to our existence."

"The war with China in the 30's came from that, I suppose."

"Well, yes. So terrible. But back to origins, Mr. Kane. While repulsing invaders, we fought amongst ourselves. In the 11th century, the samurai period began. Samurais were warriors and were hired by local leaders for protection. The most powerful of the warrior samurais became the local shoguns, who competed to rule the land, with the Emperor being relegated to religious figurehead. From the 11th to the 16th century, the country was not united. It was a nation of fiefdoms, fighting each other, and defending against invasion. Around 1600 the powerful shogun of the time, who managed to submit the country to his authority, decreed that no one would be allowed to come to Japan and no one would be allowed to leave. Isolation ensued for over 250 years, with culture and institutions developing in isolation from the rest of the world. The only foreign visitors allowed in were the Dutch, but only for trade and in a few ports. Then, in the mid-19th century, Japan began its period of modernization and openness to the rest of the world. This came about as a result of weakness of our leaders. American ships showed up at our shores, ships from Britain, Russia and other European nations as well. Conflicts broke out. The shogun of the time was overthrown and the Emperor restored to power. It is called the Meiji Restoration. In many ways, it was long overdue. For the first time, a constitution for the country was enacted, and industrialization was begun, both under the influence of the foreign presence and the ending of the restrictions of travel outside the country. At the same time, the influence and respect of the Emperor was restored."

"Which brings us to the near destruction of Japan through our aggression this last century. While this was all going on, throughout time, in conflicts with our neighbors, the Chinese, the Koreans, the Mongolians, there developed a notion of racial superiority over these other peoples. Many elites took it to extremes. This belief of superiority and of destiny to be the most powerful people of Asia led us to become the aggressor nation we became in the 1920's, 30's and 40's. The leaders of the country said it was our destiny. The Emperor went along with it. Throughout time, however, the strong influence of religion in the daily lives of the common people remained. Many elites twisted it to justify the actions to conquer and impose. But my grandfather is an example of the humble, peaceful soul of the people, despite coming from a traditional landholding family, with a tradition as well of military service."

"Your grandfather. From a traditional military family. What did he do during the war?" What has he told his family, Bob thought

"He taught people how to fly. He was an aviation instructor. He has a bad leg, which you probably noticed. He said it was injured in a flight training accident. But he refuses to talk about the war. We never ask him anymore."

"I understand. I don't talk about it either. This has been great, Kumi. I understand a lot more now. I never took the time to learn very much about Japan. I must admit, being in the war when I was young, I had no interest in revisiting anything that had to do with it. I thank you. And once again, I am glad you are part of our family."

A month later..

Robbie was on the phone with his grandfather. "Grandpa, I've got great news for you. Kumi is pregnant. We found out about it yesterday. I just informed Mom and Dad and now it's your turn to get the news."

"Well, great. Great news, Robbie. Another little Kane."

"Yes, another Kane. With that, I have a proposal for you. Kumi and I are going to Japan for a week to spend some time with her parents. She also wants to see some of her friends. With the pregnancy, it will be more difficult if we do it later. We're leaving three weeks from tomorrow. Why don't you come with us? A little vacation. We can do some visiting. You seemed to be interested in the history of Japan when we were with you. We can even go see a ballgame. Crazy baseball fans there. You have to see it. Why not, Grandpa?"

Bob thought about it for a moment before responding. "Good idea, Robbie. I'm getting older. There won't be many more chances to do this. I'm on. Book me a ticket with yours and tell me how much it costs. Good idea." Maybe I'll see my old friend, my comrade in bad memories, the bomber of my ship. I can't believe the incredible irony of this. There must be a reason why this is happening.

Chapter 25

"Where are you taking me, Robbie? What are we going to see today?" Bob was with his grandson, who had rented a car for two days to show his grandfather a bit of Japan. "First, we're going to Himeji Castle, the finest and grandest of Japan's feudal castles and an hour west of Osaka. It is an amazing complex of towers, walled enclosures, passageways and gardens, the home and redoubt of shoguns of the past. I'm sure you will enjoy seeing it, and learning about this country in the process. Then, we will come back to Osaka and go to a ballgame. Kumi's father will meet us at the game. He's a huge fan."

Bob could see that his grandson was proud of being able to introduce him to things he appreciated about the country of his spouse. "You love Japan, don't you, Robbie?"

"Yes, I do. I have come to appreciate it a lot. You were in the war against the Japanese, weren't you, Grandpa?"

"Yes, I was. It was not nice, Robbie, but it's a long time ago."

"I guess you don't want to talk about it."

"You are right. I don't. Let's enjoy our day. What is this car, by the way?"

"A special Lexus they only sell in Japan. Half minivan, half sports car. Easy to get into and out of and fun to drive. Special for you, Grandpa."

Bob and Robbie spent the better part of the day visiting the World Heritage site of the castle at Himeji. High upon a hill, the complex with over 80 buildings covering nearly 600 acres, initially built in the 14th century and completed to its current form in the 17th, towered over the plain that stretched out from the city in all directions. Through the tour they took, Bob saw examples of aspects of Japanese life that formed the character of the nation. Living quarters, kitchens, weapons and armories, stables, dungeons, apparel, places of worship, the kami of the time. These people were warriors throughout their history, he thought. Sieged. Attacked. A feudal, militaristic society of necessity. Rigor, sacrifice, discipline. It was part of them. Samurais, swords, armor. The gentle rituals of religion. of respect, stature and honor keeping it under control. Most of the time, anyway. Until their leaders unleashed it in the horror of China and their war with us.

"This is great, Robbie. I appreciate you bringing me here. This place says a lot about Japan. I'm glad we came here."

"We are going to get something to eat, now, Grandpa, something typically Japanese," said Robbie. Robbie quickly found a small restaurant on a side street. "They have what I wanted you to try. It is their specialty."

"How do you know that? Everything is in Japanese."

"The pictures," said Robbie, pointing to the numerous pictures in the window.

"And what is that specialty?"

"Okonomiyaki. A pancake with all sorts of stuff you can choose that they fry right in front of you. It's great. I had it all the time when I was here. You will like it. And we'll have a beer with it."

Bob and Robbie sat down at a large table, the center of which was one long hot plate. No one in the small restaurant spoke English. Robbie had to point to pictures of different ingredients he could find on the menu to tell the cook what he wanted for their own Okonomiyaki. The cook reached below the table, brought out a number of bowls of ingredients, a couple pieces of seafood, rapidly chopped everything up using some huge knives, mixed it all with a batter and fried it in front of them.

"This is great," said Bob after a bite or two. "What's in it?"

"Well, squid, eel, pork, kale, turnip, onion, eggs, a bunch of other vegetables as far I could tell from the picture and some spices you will never have heard of."

"Squid. Eel. Sorry I asked. Very good, just the same. Eel. I don't think you can get this in Monterey."

"No, it's not like the suchi places we're used to. Japan only. Kumi told me it came out of the war years and afterwards when people had to use whatever they had. It stuck. Now there are restaurants all over Japan that basically serve only this."

"OK, Robbie. Let's finish and get to the game."

Bob, Robbie and Kumi's father had taken their seats at Hanshin Stadium, home of the Hanshin Tigers, well in advance of the start of the game. "We're here pretty early, Robbie. Game doesn't start for another forty-five minutes."

"We came early on purpose. I wanted you to see this. Look out there." The crowds in left and right field were standing, cheering, brandishing huge flags back and forth and chanting slogans to the beat of drums. The teams were taking infield practice, the first pitch was a long way off, but the place was rocking. People in the sections behind third base were rising up and sitting down to the chants of a man with a horn standing on the roof of the dugout, urging them on.

"This is wild. Happens at every game?"

"Every game, in every park throughout Japan," said Robbie. "You should have seen it here a couple years ago when I was here. The all-Japan high school baseball championship. Forty-five thousand people going nuts. High school. I couldn't believe it. They take this seriously. This stadium was built for that, many years ago."

"This doesn't happen back home. Lay back, relax, watch the game, appreciate the fine points of the game, rise up at a home run. Nobody at infield practice whipping up the crowd. This is something."

"Baseball is part of us now," said Robbie's father-in-law. "Our American side, one could say, but with our type of involvement. Japanese can get emotional about things. Baseball is one of those. Did you know that it is the most popular sport in Japan?"

"No, I knew it was played here, but the most popular? No. When did it all start? Probably not before the war. How did it come here?"

"Well, it was before the war, Mr.Kane. It was introduced as a school sport in the 1870's by an American teacher at one of our academies. It spread across all of Japan, as a school sport and is still very prominent as such. Robbie mentioned the high school championship. It is very big. The first professional league started in the 1930's. Some of your stars, including Babe Ruth and Lou Gehrig, came to Japan in 1934 for an exhibition series against a Japanese team. It was very popular. So, baseball has been here for a long time. We have much in common with Americans, as you must know."

"Yes, I guess we do. Baseball. I had no idea."

"Business as well. We are a long way from our troubles of half a century ago."

"Yes, I believe we are," replied Bob, looking off into center field.

Chapter 26

"I didn't bomb your ship. One of my men did. I flew over right after." Bob and Keiji were in the garden of Keiji's home in Kyoto.

"But it was your squadron. You were the commander," said Bob.

"Yes, I was. Bob, do you think I am happy to go over this? Do you think I was happy that day? I was not."

"What did you do after that? After that day?

"I tried to forget it. I was made some sort of hero. I was no hero in my mind."

"But what did you do the rest of the war? December 7 was day one."

"A few months later, my carrier was at Midway. It was sunk along with three others. I was in the air when it happened and my plane was shot down. I was hit in the leg and rescued, but I could no longer be an active bomber pilot. They made me an instructor on the mainland. It's what I did the rest of the war."

"Taught kamikazes to be kamikazes, right?"

"Bob, I was appalled by it all. I was no hero. I did what I had to do, and not blemish the honor of my father. I have spent the rest of my life atoning for the horror and carnage of that day."

"I'm sorry, Keiji. I did not intend to go there. I'm sorry. I have fought all my life with the memory of that day. I despised your people for sixty years. That is changing. Please forgive me."

"I have an idea, Bob. I want you to see how I spend my days. Come to the shrine tomorrow. I will show you the meaning for my life and the essence of what it has been for me for fifty years. It will do you good. I guarantee it."

"How should I dress?"

"Just the way you are now."

Bob and Keiji were on a terrace in the shade of cherry trees behind the shrine. No one else was around. Keiji had explained what his days were like as a priest. Bob had listened and had accepted to have tea. "I never drink tea, Keiji. But I'm here. Your life is so different from mine. This meeting you here, even being in Japan, is so far from what I ever thought I would be doing. My grandson has showed me around the last two days. I have learned a lot, have come to appreciate the history of the country, of the people. I understand more now what led to that day so long ago."

"What led to that day was the loss of our soul. Our leaders betrayed it. I knew then, after the attack, I would someday have to confront what we had done. Someday, somehow. It was always with me. But I never thought it would be with someone from the ship we sank. Never," Keiji said.

"We are two old men who have two things in common. One, a day and its carnage that changed our lives and the other a union of our offspring. Which one shall dominate in our dealings with each other? Can we talk about it?"

"If you wish. What did you feel toward me that day on the beach in California?" asked Keiji.

"Hate. Anger. I wanted to explode. I almost did. Then…"

"Then what?"

"Your face. Your tears…..I recognized at that moment that your grief could be, was, as great as mine. Only someone who had been there and haunted by it could have the same reaction. I saw it in your eyes. I wanted to explode, but I couldn't."

"It was difficult. Painful. I was crumbling with what was coming back to me. I did not want to go as far as I did. I could not take it back. It rolled out of me. I wanted to go back to the restaurant, to the hotel, to the airport, home. Undo all that had brought me to that moment on the beach. I was caught. I told you. That morning came back to me. It was too much. I had to say it. Sixty years….bottled up inside. It came out. If you would have struck me, I would have taken it," said Keiji. "Punishment…..but you did not."

"I couldn't…." Bob hesitated for a moment, looked out across the garden away from Keiji, then continued without looking at him. "One last time, Keiji. One last talk about that day. What did you see that morning?"

"The end of Japan. The travesty of what we were doing. I saw the destruction of us. I knew that it would come, as I flew low over the water. The men in the water, the bodies, the fires everywhere. Japan had signed its death warrant. It nearly happened."

"Did you tell anybody?"

"Only my wife many months later. I could not share any of that with anyone else. But I was finished as a warrior. A shot from one of your planes at Midway ended it a few months later. Mercifully. Shall we go on, Bob?"

"Yes, if you want to. It is liberating. Secrets of a lifetime that you don't dare expose to others, particularly your loved ones. My first wife knew, she was at Pearl Harbor. I told my oldest son before he died. I have a friend, a dear friend who was on the Arizona with me and survived, albeit with terrible burns to his whole body. He made something of his life, despite the disfigurement and we are close to this day. He is the only one I have really spoken to about that day. And a therapist many years later." Bob hesitated, then looked over at his host. "Your life became one of spirituality. Mine was one of nightmares and missed opportunities to get closer to my loved ones. It took the death of my son to get me to deal with it."

"That day. Where were you?"

"I was on deck, doing something that was somebody else's responsibility. I was there because I had met my future wife the day before, on the beach, and I was in love, couldn't sleep, the thought of her kept me awake. I had to do something. So I was up on the deck when your planes came across the water and it all exploded. That woman, the love of my life, who I only tracked down after the war, saved my life that day. I was injured, burned, and had a cracked skull. In the water and swam to the island next to the ship. You came along the water, you say, after the explosion."

"Yes. To check what had been done."

"You probably saw me. I saw you. I thought about that after the day on the beach. The lone plane flying low over the wreckage, not shooting, with the big bomb underneath. The memory of it came back. It was you."

"It was me."

"You know, the why it all happened. I was here, at the end of the war, in Kobe. I hated it. I had no sympathy for anyone. I wanted to kill people, flush them away with all the debris, more than I wanted to help them. I met a man walking one day, in the midst of the destruction, the rubble, the twisted and charred remains of buildings. He was looking straight ahead, ignoring me. I said something to him, about the stupidity of the war, not expecting him to understand a word of what I was saying. He replied in perfect English. 'It was our destiny' and continued on his way, without looking at me or changing the pace of his walk."

"It was our destiny. My father told me the same before he died. A broken, disillusioned man. He believed the lie."

"What lie?"

174

"Our destiny to rule. To be the masters of Asia, the Pacific and the Orient, to have all the other peoples subservient to the wisdom and might of the Empire of Japan. To push America back to its own shores, never to intrude on our domination of this half of the world. First China, then America, then Russia. He believed it. He died two months before the end of the war. I can see the man who you met on that street in Kobe. I can see it happening. It could well have been my father."

"So what do we do from here?" asked Bob.

"Bury our nightmares, love our children, share whatever wisdom we have gained."

"Yes. But I mean you and I, these two old men with a strange, unbelievable story that we don't want anybody else to know."

"We are united now, whether we like it or not. We could have a respectful friendship, even a warm one beyond blood and family. You may always hate me and I would understand. But I don't hate you and I'm sorry for what we did. You will always be welcome in my home."

"I respect you for that, Keiji. The incredible connection ….it defies belief…. but let us make the best of it. I don't know what else to say."

"Maybe friends?"

"Yes, friends. I think we could. Just one thing, though. We should keep our connection to that day from our families."

"Yes. Only between us."

Chapter 27

"David, this is Maria, your father's housekeeper." Before David could respond, the lady continued. "Your father is not well. He collapsed this morning just after I arrived. I called for an ambulance. They just left. They said they were taking him to Monterey City Hospital. I think you should come."

"I see. Of course, I will be going. As soon as I can. I knew this day would come. What was his condition when they left?"

"He was unconscious but breathing. They immediately put him in the ambulance. I don't know any more."

"Ok. I will call the hospital. Luciana and I will be there later, as soon as we can get a flight. I have a key to the house. Thank you, Maria. You have been very good to my father."

"Let me know what happens. Here is the number at my home."

Later that evening, at the hospital..

"Mr. Kane, your father had an aneurism. He is unconscious, in a coma and we are not sure he will come out of it. He is not responding to stimuli. His kidneys are failing as well. It does not look good."

"He's 83. Old age, doctor?"

"You could say that, although he looked to be in pretty good shape for 83. The last checkup with his physician, who was here earlier, was only three months ago and nothing alarming had showed up."

David went to Bob's room. He looked at his father. Everything looked normal. The strong, tanned face, hands stretched out at his side, the forearms with the scars. We never really talked about that, thought David. A tube from a monitor connected to his arm. Just a man asleep.

"Dad, can you hear me?" Nothing. David took his hand, squeezed it. Nothing. "Dad, can you hear me? Squeeze my hand." Nothing.

The next morning while having breakfast before going to the hospital, David heard a knock on the front door. It was the housekeeper. "I couldn't stay away, Mr. Kane. How is your father doing?"

"Come in, come in, Maria. My father is unconscious, in a coma, not responding. It does not look good, but do come in. My wife and I are getting ready to go to the hospital."

"Mr. Kane, given what you have told me about his condition, I have something to tell you upon his instructions. There is an envelope he put in a drawer of the table in his bedroom. He told me to give it to you in case anything happened to him. He wanted to make sure you found it."

"When did he tell you this?" David asked as they made their way to his father's bedroom.

"A few months ago, after he came back from Japan with your son."

David opened the envelope. It was a letter addressed to him.

David, this will hopefully help you understand your father. It is also a request. I am a survivor of the sinking of the battleship USS Arizona at Pearl Harbor on December 7, 1941. I have kept it from you all your life. For better or for worse. Please do not hold it against me. I have felt guilty about being a survivor every day since that day. I lived, over a thousand of my crewmates and friends did not. I had a life, they didn't. I have decided to join them in death out of honor and respect for them. My ashes are to be placed in the hull of the Arizona, among the remains of what is left of the over one thousand men who never made it out. Twenty of my fellow survivors have decided to do the same, including my lifelong friend and crewmate, Davey Poole, after whom you are named. I hope you understand. This is not a betrayal of my love for your mother or your brother. They would understand. You are to take a portion of my ashes, put them in a separate urn and bury them next to the graves of your mother and John at the cemetery in Kansas City, with whatever gravestone you find appropriate. I want that there, even if a major portion of my ashes are buried at Pearl Harbor. Contact the Arizona Survivor's Association, address attached, to ask them how to arrange for the placement of the ashes in the remains of the ship. They can put my name on the plaque at the Memorial. You will know what I mean when you are there. Please follow my instructions, David. I love you, your lovely Luciana, and your children, my wonderful grandchildren. Dad

David was at the hospital, in the room with his father. "Dad, if you hear me, I understand. I read your letter. I will do as you ask. I understand why you never told me about your time in the war. Just the same, I wish I could have known. We could have been closer. I wish it could have been. But you have been a great dad." He squeezed his father's hand. He thought he detected a small squeeze in return. He wasn't sure. "Goodbye, Dad, if you must go. Go in peace."

Six weeks later..

It was a beautiful sunny day at Pearl Harbor, with the water surrounding the memorial shimmering in the sunlight and a light breeze coming in from the ocean.

David had taken the launch from the mainland to the memorial with the urn carrying his father's ashes an hour before. He was to meet with the commander of the base who would preside over the ceremony, the color guard administering the four gun salute and the Navy diver who was to lower the container with the urn into the hull. While the Navy personnel were preparing the ceremony, David took in the full serenity of the emplacement – the submerged remains of the massive ship over six hundred feet long and one hundred feet wide, the Memorial straddling over it, the huge white marble plaque on the end wall with the names of the 1,177 men of the ship who had died that day, and the smaller one with the names of the twenty men who, like his father, had decided to place their ashes in the ship below. Before he had taken the launch to the Memorial, he had watched the film shown to all visitors in the small theatre at the dock. The film showed footing of the days before the attack with servicemen and women enjoying afternoons on the beach, and evenings dancing to the tunes of the popular big bands of the time, not having any idea of what was coming, then the films of the attack itself and the descriptions of the destruction. This is what he went through, thought David. No wonder he never wanted to talk about it.

The ceremony was ready to begin. The launch with another group of fifty people had landed. People could see that something was about to begin. The commander of the base called for attention and silence. The crowd gathered around the center of the open-sided memorial. The urn with Bob Kane's ashes was on a table next to the commander, draped with the Stars and Stripes.

"Ladies and gentlemen, we are committing to the deep this morning, the remains of Lieutenant Robert Kane, United States Navy, crewman and survivor of the sinking of the USS Arizona on December 7, 1941. At his request, his ashes are being placed with the remains of his comrades in arms who never made it out and whose remains were never recovered. The act of Lieutenant Kane is one of respect and honor to the memory of his comrades who made the supreme sacrifice in defense of their country but never had the chance to live the life he led. May God have mercy on his soul. I ask you for a moment of silence."

At the conclusion of the moment of silence, the commander took the urn from the table, gave it to David, then ordered the officer at arms to proceed with the salute. "Ready!" The sailors in white raised their rifles over the bow of the submerged hull, then the "Fire!" order came. The sailors fired, lowered their rifles, then repeated the process three more times. David then handed the urn to the Navy diver, who placed it in a small container and lowered himself to the opening in the hull below the surface.

As the diver was placing the urn and the crowd was dispersing as the formal ceremony was over, David observed a small elderly man at the railing, dressed in a gray three quarter length robe worn over a suit and tie with a gold sash draped around his shoulders, bowing in the direction of the operation below with his hands together in a gesture of prayer. The man rose up, bowed again, keeping his head low, maintaining his position for what seemed to be a minute or more. David watched. Some other people watched as well, but most had turned to complete their guided tour of the facility and were not aware of what was happening at the railing. The base commander and the other Navy personnel had retreated to the closed end of the structure. As David watched, the elderly man rose up, looked out over the harbor and the mountains beyond, lingering for a long moment as he observed the surroundings, then turned to where David could see his face. It was Kumi's grandfather. He quickly approached the man who turned and bowed to David when he saw him approaching.

"Sir, I had no idea you were coming. I had no idea you even knew."

"I decided to come, David. To pay my respects. I liked your father very much. He was a fine man."

"How did you know? About this?

"Kumi. She said you were here. To do this."

"It was supposed to be a secret. Only to the family."

"Well, David, I am family. I came to honor a member, your father. To say a prayer. It was important that I do this. May his soul rest in peace."

"You know why he did this."

"Of course. As the officer said, out of honor and respect for his comrades."

As they returned to the mainland in the launch, David observed his daughter-in-law's's grandfather looking out over the harbor, turning to view it all as well as the mountains in the distance, seemingly oblivious to David's presence.

"Sir, you look like you have been here before. Have you?"

The old man hesitated, looking off across the water. "No. I have never been here before," he replied, without taking his gaze away from the water and the mountains in the distance.

"Did you know about this, about my father here? Before this?"

"No. I did not."

Other novels by the author

www.tomcreary.com

www.ingramcontent.com/pod-product-compliance
Lightning Source LLC
Chambersburg PA
CBHW071213260626
47162CB00004B/1279